LOVE & MARRIAGE

Celebrate Harlequin's fiftieth anniversary
in style with two brand-new stories
from two of our most popular
Harlequin Romance® authors:

BETTY NEELS

MAKING SURE OF SARAH

"Once again Betty Neels perfects another hero
to pine over..."
—*Romantic Times* on **A SECRET INFATUATION**

"favorite author..."
—*Romantic Times*

EMMA GOLDRICK

SOMETHING BLUE

"The enormously talented Emma Goldrick dishes
up a keeper for our bookshelves."
—*Romantic Times* on **THE BABY CAPER**

"A madcap, high jinx read that will keep you
laughing throughout the entire book..."
—*Rendezvous* on **THE BABY CAPER**

Betty Neels spent her childhood and youth in Devonshire, England, before training as a nurse and midwife. She was an army nursing sister during the war, married a Dutchman and subsequently lived in Holland for fourteen years. She now lives with her husband in Dorset, and has a daughter and grandson. Her hobbies are reading, animals, old buildings and writing. Betty started to write on retirement from nursing, incited by a lady in a library bemoaning the lack of romantic novels.

Emma Goldrick was born and raised in Puerto Rico, where she met and married her husband, Bob, a career military man. Thirty years and four children later they retired and took up nursing and teaching. In 1980 they turned to collaborative writing. After sixty years of living over half the world, and a full year of studying the Harlequin Romance® style, their first submission was accepted. Between them they have written over forty books. Emma's hobbies include grandchildren, flower gardens, reading and travel. Sadly, in 1996, Bob Goldrick passed away. Emma continues to write in his memory.

Betty Neels
Emma Goldrick

Love &
Marriage

HARLEQUIN®

TORONTO • NEW YORK • LONDON
AMSTERDAM • PARIS • SYDNEY • HAMBURG
STOCKHOLM • ATHENS • TOKYO • MILAN • MADRID
PRAGUE • WARSAW • BUDAPEST • AUCKLAND

ISBN 0-373-03554-3

LOVE & MARRIAGE

Copyright © 1999 by Harlequin Books S.A.

The publisher acknowledges the copyright holders of the individual works as follows:

MAKING SURE OF SARAH
Copyright © 1999 by Betty Neels

SOMETHING BLUE
Copyright © 1992 by Emma Goldrick

Contents

Making Sure of Sarah
Betty Neels

CHAPTER ONE

SARAH looked out of the car's windows at the flat, peaceful countryside of Holland, no longer listening to her stepfather's angry voice blaming everyone and everything but himself for getting lost. Her mother, sitting beside him with the map, had been ignored when she had pointed out the road they should have taken, but the main butt of his ill humour was Sarah.

He turned his red, angry face and said over his shoulder, 'You must have known that we had taken a wrong turning—why didn't you say so?'

Sarah said in her quiet voice, 'I don't know Holland. I came with you and Mother because you wanted someone who could speak French while you were in France.' She added before he could reply, 'If you had told us that you intended going back home through Belgium and Holland I would have bought a Dutch dictionary—so that I could have asked the way,' she pointed out in a matter-of-fact voice.

'Don't annoy your father, dear,' said her mother.

'He isn't my father; he's my stepfather,' said Sarah, and she wondered why her mother, after ten years or more, could bear to be married to him, and why she expected Sarah to think of him as her father. It had been mutual dislike at first sight, but her mother, who had managed to go through life turning a blind eye to anything which upset her, had steadfastly pretended that her ill-tempered husband and the daughter she had never quite understood were the best of friends.

Then, because she loved her mother, Sarah added, 'There

9

was a road sign a mile or so back. It said "Arnhem, seventeen kilometres".'

'Why didn't you say so?' asked her stepfather furiously. 'Letting me drive miles out of my way.'

'I did. You told me not to bother you.'

He drove on then, muttering under his breath. Sarah turned a deaf ear, vaguely aware of her mother's conciliatory murmurs, uneasy now since he was driving much too fast. The road was narrow, with a ditch on either side and fields beyond; it stretched ahead of them with nothing in sight and the March day was drawing to a close. She thanked heaven silently that there were no curves or corners, and no traffic at all.

She had overlooked the ditches. Her stepfather, never a good driver, and an even worse one when he was in a bad temper, took a hand off the wheel to snatch the map from his wife's lap, and the car shot over the narrow grass verge and tumbled into the ditch.

The ditch was half filled with water draining from the fields, and the car hit the muddy bottom with tremendous force, its bonnet completely buried.

Sarah, flung hither and thither and ending up rather the worse for wear, still in her seat belt, was too shocked to speak, but it was, in a way, reassuring to hear her stepfather swearing, and then shouting, 'Get me out, get me out!'

Typical! thought Sarah, light-headed. What about Mother…? She came to then, scrambling round until she could undo the belt and lean over the seat where her mother was. Her mother was slumped over, her head against the dashboard, and she didn't answer when Sarah spoke to her. Sarah leaned over and found her arm and felt for her pulse—beating, she was relieved to find, reasonably strong. Her stepfather gave another shout, and she said loudly, 'Be quiet, do. Get out and help Mother, she's hurt…'

'You stupid girl. *I'm* hurt—my leg, my chest. Never

mind your mother for the moment, go and get help. Be quick. Heaven knows how badly injured I am.'

'This is your fault,' said Sarah, 'and all you can think of is that you're hurt. Well, so is Mother...'

She wriggled out of her seat, and after a struggle managed to open the door of the car. The water, icy cold and thick with mud, came up to her knees, but she hardly noticed that. It was late afternoon and the sky was grey, but there was still plenty of light. She tugged at the handle of the door by her mother and found it jammed, so got back into the car again and leaned over to open it from inside. It didn't budge.

Frantically she managed to undo her mother's seat belt and haul her gently into a more comfortable position, relieved to feel her pulse was stronger now. There were rugs in the boot, but first she must turn off the engine, still running, and take a look at her stepfather. She hung over the back of his seat and managed to undo his seat belt and sit him up a little, not listening to his roars of rage.

And all this had taken only a few minutes, she realised, edging her way round to the boot and finding it thankfully burst open and the rugs easy to reach. She tucked them round her mother and stepfather and then scrambled up the bank and took a look. The flat countryside stretched round her, wide fields divided by ditches, a few trees, and not a house in sight. There was a clump of larger trees some way off. Perhaps there would be a farm there, but surely even on this quiet road there would be traffic or something, someone...

There was; still far off, but coming towards her, was a horse and cart. Sarah shouted then, and waved and shouted again until she was hoarse, but the cart didn't increase its speed. She didn't dare to leave her mother and stepfather, and watched it in an agony of impatience as the beast plodded steadily towards her. When the cart was near enough she ran towards it.

The man holding the reins halted the horse and stared down at her.

'An accident,' said Sarah. 'Police, ambulance, hospital.' And, since he didn't seem to understand her, she said it all again and added, 'Please, hurry…'

The man had a broad, dull face but he looked kind. He looked across at the upended car and then back at Sarah. *'Politie?'*

'Yes, yes. Please, hurry…'

He nodded then, thought for a moment, and broke into speech. It was a pity that she couldn't understand a word of it, but he ended with the word *politie* and urged his horse forward. Sarah watched the cart disappear slowly into the distance until the clump of trees hid it from view, and then she climbed back into the ditch.

Her mother was moaning a little, and Sarah tucked the rug more tightly around her and contrived to shift her legs so that they were free of the cold water which filled the front of the car. She tried to do the same for her stepfather, but one leg was at an awkward angle and she didn't dare to touch it. She made him as comfortable as possible and climbed out of the ditch once more, to meet a heartening sight: the blue flashing lights of a police car coming at speed.

The two men in it were large, reassuringly calm, and spoke English. She wanted to fling herself on a broad chest and burst into tears of relief, but it didn't seem the right moment.

'My mother and stepfather are in the car,' she told them, in a voice which shook only slightly. 'They're hurt. Is an ambulance coming?'

'It comes at once. And you, miss? You are not hurt?' the older of the two officers asked her.

'No, I'm fine.' She peered anxiously over the edge of the ditch to where the other officer was bending over her mother. She would have joined him, but the ambulance arrived then and she was urged to stand on one side while the policemen and the paramedics began the task of getting her mother and stepfather out of the car.

They were hefty men, and made short work of breaking down the car door, releasing her mother and lifting her into the ambulance. Getting her stepfather out was more difficult. His leg was broken and he was cut by broken glass, moreover he disputed their actions, shouting and swearing. Sarah was sorry that he was injured, but she hoped that the men would put his uninhibited behaviour down to shock.

It was almost dark now. While they had been busy, Sarah had unloaded their cases from the boot and stood with them, waiting to be told what to do next.

'You will come with us to the hospital,' said the older constable. 'We will take your luggage to the police station and tomorrow you may come and fetch it.' He waved the ambulance away and opened the car door for her. 'You have everything, passports, money?'

'Yes, I've put them in one of the cases. Where are we going?'

'Arnhem.' He gave her a brief glance. 'You are OK?'

Sarah said, 'Yes, thank you.' She was alive, unhurt, although she was aware of aches and pains and wet and icy feet and legs; she was OK.

The hospital at Arnhem was large and modern, and the Accident Room was heaving with people. The two policemen set her down beside the ambulance, warned her to collect the cases from the police station in the morning and be ready to give a report of the accident, and sped on their way. She watched them go with regret; they had been briskly friendly—warning her stepfather that they would come to the hospital to see him in the morning, patting her on the shoulder in a kindly fashion—and now they had gone, siren sounding, blue lights flashing. Another accident?

Sarah followed the two stretchers into the hospital and presently found herself in a waiting room with a lot of other anxious people. Someone would come and report on her mother and stepfather, she was told by a busy nurse, taking down particulars and thankfully speaking English.

Sarah settled into one of the plastic chairs arranged around the room. Her feet were numb now, and she smelled horrible. A cup of tea, she thought longingly, and a nice warm bath and then bed. She was hungry, too, and she felt guilty about that with her mother and stepfather injured. People came and went. Slowly the room emptied. Surely someone would come for her soon. She closed her eyes on a daydream of endless pots of tea and plates piled high with hot buttered toast and slept.

Mr ter Breukel, consultant orthopaedic surgeon at the hospital, finished his examination of Mr Holt's leg and bent his massive person over his patient. He studied the ill-tempered face and listened patiently to the diatribe directed at himself, his staff and everyone in general.

When Mr Holt drew breath, he said quietly, 'You have a broken leg; it will need to be pinned and plated. You have two broken ribs, a sprained wrist, and superficial cuts and bruises. You will be put to bed presently and in the morning I will set the leg. You will need to stay here until it is considered expedient to return you to England.'

Mr Holt said furiously, 'I demand to be sent to England immediately. How am I to know that you are competent to deal with my injuries? I am a businessman and have some influential friends.'

Mr ter Breukel ignored the rudeness. 'I will see you in

the morning. Your wife will be warded also. She has concussion but is not seriously hurt.'

He waited for Mr Holt to say something, and when he didn't added, 'Was there anyone else with you?'

'My stepdaughter.' Mr Holt gave him a look of deep dislike. 'She's quite capable of taking care of herself.'

'In the circumstances,' said Mr ter Breukel, 'that is most fortunate.'

The Accident Room was emptying, so he could safely leave the minor cases to the two casualty officers on duty, but first he supposed he should find this stepdaughter. Probably with her mother...

Mrs Holt was fully conscious now, and complaining weakly. She had no wish to stay in hospital; she must have a private room, she wanted her own nightclothes, her own toiletries...

Mr ter Breukel bent over the stretcher, lifted a limp hand and took her pulse. It was steady and quite strong. 'Your daughter?' he asked quietly. 'She was with you in the car?'

'Yes, yes, of course. Where is she? Why isn't she here with me? She knows how bad my nerves are. Someone must fetch her. She must find a good hotel where I can stay for a few days until my husband can return to England.'

'Mr Holt will have to remain here for some time, Mrs Holt, and I cannot allow you to leave this hospital until you have recovered from a slight concussion.'

'How tiresome.' Mrs Holt turned her head away and closed her eyes.

Mr ter Breukel nodded to the porters to wheel her away to the ward and went in search of the third member of the party.

The place was quieter now, and the waiting room was empty save for Sarah. He stood looking at her—such an ordinary girl, dirty and dishevelled, a bruise on one cheek and smelling vilely of the mud clinging to her person. A girl without looks, pale, her hair hanging in untidy damp streamers around a face which could easily pass unnoticed in a crowd. A girl completely lacking in glamour.

He sighed deeply; to fall in love at first sight with this malodorous sleeping girl, with, as far as he could see, no pretentions to beauty or even good looks, was something he had not expected. But falling in love, he had always understood, was unpredictable, and, as far as he was concerned, irrevocable. That they hadn't exchanged a word, nor spoken, made no difference. He, heartwhole until that minute, and with no intention of marrying until it suited him, had lost that same heart.

But he wasn't a callow youth; he would have to tread softly, otherwise he might lose her. He went close to her chair and said gently, 'Miss Holt?'

Sarah opened her eyes and allowed them to travel up a vast expanse of superfine clerical grey cloth, past a richly sombre tie and white linen, until they reached his face.

She said clearly, 'Not Miss Holt; he's my stepfather. Beckwith—Sarah Beckwith. That's a nice tie—Italian silk?'

Mr ter Breukel, aware that she wasn't quite awake yet, agreed gravely that it was Italian silk. Her eyes, he saw with delight, were quite beautiful, a vivid dark blue, veiled by mousy lashes.

Sarah sat up straight and pushed her hair off her face. 'I'm sorry, I fell asleep.' She studied his face, a very trustworthy face, she decided, as well as a handsome one, with its high-bridged nose and firm mouth and heavy-lidded eyes. 'Mother...?'

'I am Litrik ter Breukel, consultant orthopaedic surgery. I'm sorry there was no one to see you. It has been a busy evening. Your mother is to stay here for a few days. She has been concussed, but should recover quickly. There are one or two cuts and bruises which will heal quickly. Your stepfather has a broken leg, fractured ribs, and he has been cut by glass. He must remain until he is fit to be sent back to England.'

'Do I have to arrange that?'

'No, no. We will see to that at the appropriate time.'

'May I see Mother?'

'Of course. But first I think you must be checked to make sure that you have no injuries. And you will need a tetanus injection and to be cleaned up.'

'I'm not hurt, only dirty and a bit scratched. And I smell dreadful…'

She went without demur to the Accident Room, where he handed her over to a stout, middle-aged woman with a kind face and a harassed manner. She spoke English, too. Sarah submitted to being cleaned up, her scratches and bruises dealt with, her injection given, to the accompaniment of her companion's pleased astonishment that she wasn't more seriously injured, and then, looking clean and smelling of good soap, she was handed back to Mr ter Breukel, who, eyeing her with all the delight of a man in love, thought she looked like some small girl who had been run through the mangle and left to dry.

He said merely, 'You feel better now? We will go to your mother.' And he led the way through the hospital, in and out of lifts, up and down staircases, and eventually into a ward with a dozen beds in it.

Her mother had a corner bed, and was lying back comfortably, but when she saw Sarah she asked peevishly, 'Where have you been? I feel terrible. I'm sure that I'm a good deal worse than these doctors say. You should have been here with me…'

Sarah said gently, 'I'm sorry, Mother. I fell asleep…'

'Asleep? You must have known that I was lying here in pain? And your poor father…'

'Stepfather,' said Sarah.

'Yes, well—it is all very well for you, you don't appear
to have been hurt in the least.' She added fretfully, 'I knew
this would happen; you always manage to annoy him.'

Sarah said nothing to that, and her mother closed her
eyes. 'Now go away and spare a thought for your poor
mother before you go to sleep in a comfortable bed.'

Sarah bent and kissed an averted cheek, and then was
led away by Mr ter Breukel, who had been standing just
behind her, listening to every word.

He made no mention of their conversation, however, but
walked her silently to the entrance, where she stopped and
offered her hand. 'You've been very kind. Thank you. I
know my mother and stepfather will be all right here. May
I come and see them in the morning?'

He had no intention of letting her go, and for once a
kindly Fate lent a helping hand; Sarah gave a small choking
gasp. 'I'm going to be sick...'

There was a providential sink nearby, and she found herself leaning over it, a firm, cool hand holding her head...

Presently she gasped, 'Oh, the relief,' and then, aware of
the hand, mumbled, 'How awful for you. I'm so sorry.'

'Best thing you could have done. You probably swallowed a good deal of ditchwater.'

He bent over her, wiped her face with his handkerchief
and led her outside into the crisp March evening.

Sarah tugged on an arm to call a halt. 'Thank you,' she
said again. 'I'm fine now.'

'You have somewhere to go? Money? Do you know your
way about Arnhem?'

She looked away, searching for an answer which
wouldn't sound like a fib.

'The police said I could collect our cases and things in
the morning from the police station...'

'You know where that is?'

'No, but I can ask.'

'And until morning?' he persisted.

She opened her mouth to utter something misleading but convincing.

'No, no. Let us have no nonsense. You have no money, no clothes, you are extremely dirty and probably hungry. You will come home with me...'

He spoke pleasantly, but he sounded as though he meant it. All the same, she said tartly, 'Indeed I won't.'

Mr ter Breukel slid effortlessly into his bedside manner. 'My dear young lady, my sister will be delighted to meet you, and help you in any way she can.' He didn't smile, but Sarah, peeping at him, had to admit that he looked—she sought the right word—safe.

'If you're sure I won't be a nuisance, thank you.'

He nodded, walked to where a dark grey Rolls Royce was parked and popped her neatly into it, got in beside her and drove away.

After a moment Sarah asked, 'Will I be able to arrange for Mother to go home soon? If she isn't seriously hurt...'

'Shall we leave that for the moment? Time enough when you have seen the police in the morning. You will probably have to make a statement, as will your parents. Once the matter has been dealt with, arrangements can be made for you to return to England.'

He drove to the city's heart, where there were still ancient houses and shops which had miraculously escaped damage during the terrific battle towards the end of World War II, stopping presently in a narrow, canal-lined street.

The houses in it were old, narrow and tall, leaning against each other, each with a splendid gable. He stopped the car halfway down, got out and opened the door for Sarah. She got out and looked around her. She could have stepped back into the seventeenth century, for there was no traffic, no cars parked, only the rustle of trees lining the canal to break the stillness.

'You live here?'

'Yes.' He took her arm and marched her across the narrow pavement and up some worn steps to a handsome door flanked by long narrow windows on either side of it. He unlocked the door and urged her gently before him into the narrow hall beyond, its walls panelled, black and white tiles underfoot, a brass chandelier, probably as old as the house, hanging from the beautiful plaster ceiling.

As they entered, a door at the end of the hall opened, and a short, stout man came to meet them. He was accompanied by a large dog with small yellow eyes and a thick grey pelt, who bared awesome teeth in what Sarah hoped was a smile. Apparently it was, for he pranced up to Mr ter Breukel and offered his head for a scratch with reassuring meekness.

Mr ter Breukel obliged, exchanged a few words with the man and switched to English. 'This is Jaap; he and his wife look after me. And this is Max; he looks fierce, but he has the disposition of a lamb.'

Sarah shook Jaap's hand, then patted Max's woolly head and tried not to notice the teeth before she was propelled gently through a door into a high-ceilinged room with narrow windows and a hooded fireplace. She had no time to see more than that before a young woman got up from a chair by the cheerful fire and came to meet them.

'Litrik, you're late.' She lifted a face for his kiss and smiled at Sarah.

'Suzanne, this is Sarah Beckwith. She and her parents had a car accident this afternoon. They are at St Bravo's and she has agreed to stay here with us for the night. The police have all their things, and it is rather late to find a hotel...'

Suzanne took Sarah's hand. 'How horrid for you, and we'll love to have you; you must be feeling awful.' She cast a discreet eye over Sarah's deplorable person. 'Would you like a bath before dinner? Anneke can get your clothes cleaned up while I lend you something to wear.'

She took Sarah's arm. 'This is fun—not for you, of course, but I'm so pleased you're here. We'll find Anneke and I'll take you upstairs.'

She turned to her brother. 'Dinner in half an hour? You don't have to go back this evening?'

'No, not unless something turns up.' He gave a casual nod and smile and went to the fire, and Sarah, reassured by the matter-of-fact air he was careful to maintain, went back into the hall and up a carved staircase in a recess halfway down it.

A small, thin woman was waiting for them when they reached the landing.

'This is Anneke,' said Suzanne. 'Jaap's wife and a family friend for years and years.'

Sarah offered a hand once more and was aware that she was being carefully studied from beady brown eyes. Then Anneke smiled and led the way down a passage leading off the landing, opened a door and waved Suzanne and Sarah into the room beyond.

A charming room of pale pastel colours, deeply carpeted, with curtained windows a froth of white muslin. Sarah paused on the threshold. 'My filthy shoes…' She took them off and Anneke took them from her with a smile and said something to Suzanne.

'Take everything off and have a bath. Anneke will see to your things and I'll bring you some clothes.' She studied Sarah's small person. 'We're almost the same size. A sweater and trousers?' She gave Sarah a little push. 'Anneke's running a bath for you; I'll be back in ten minutes.'

Left alone, Sarah shed her damp and dirty clothes, laid them tidily on a towel so as not to spoil the carpet or quilt, and got into the bath. It was blissfully hot and delightfully

scented. She could have stayed there for hours, but
Suzanne, calling from the open door into the bedroom,
roused her.

'I've put some things on the bed. Something is bound to
fit, more or less. Dinner in ten minutes.'

Sarah, wrapped in a vast white towel, went to have a
look. There was a heap of coloured sweaters, a couple of
pairs of trousers, gossamer undies, slippers...

Dressed, her hair still damp and tied back in an untidy
plait for lack of ribbons or pins, the trousers on the large
side and the pink sweater she had chosen shrouding her
person, she took a final look at her reflection. She looked
as plain as always, she decided, but at least she was clean
and smelling sweet.

She went downstairs and found Jaap in the hall, waiting
for her. He led her with a fatherly air back into the drawing
room and Mr ter Breukel got up out of his chair and crossed
the room with just the right air of a polite host ready to put
an unexpected guest at ease.

Suzanne, watching him, hid a smile. Litrik, impervious
to the charms of various young ladies that his family, anxious for him to marry, had produced, was showing interest
in this nice little creature with the plain face and the lovely
eyes. And the pink sweater suited her very well...

Sarah, accepting a chair and a glass of sherry, happily
unaware of Suzanne's thoughts, made polite conversation
with her host and hostess, and, encouraged by Mr ter
Breukel's artless questioning, said that no, she had never
been to Arnhem before, had never been in Holland—only
her stepfather had wanted to return to England by the night
ferry to Harwich.

'Ah, yes—you live somewhere along the east coast? By
far the easiest way to return.'

'He has a house near Clapham Common—that's
London,' said Sarah flatly. And, since his raised eyebrows

invited more than that, added, 'We—that is, Mother and Father, before he died, and me...' She paused. Perhaps it was 'I'. 'We used to live in a small village in Berkshire.'

'Delightful country,' murmured Mr ter Breukel, inviting further confidences.

'Yes, quite different from Clapham Common.'

'You live at home?'

'Yes. Mother isn't very strong...'

Suzanne asked, 'You're not getting married or anything like that?'

'No, we—I don't go out much.'

Mr ter Breukel said easily, 'One never knows what awaits one round the corner.' He knew, of course, but patience was something of which he had plenty. Having found her, he wasn't going to lose her by being hasty.

Jaap came to tell them that dinner was served; Suzanne took his arm and they crossed the hall to the dining room, with its panelled walls and oval table, the George the First Oak dresser along one wall, the oak Chippendale chairs. A pair of crystal candelabra stood on the dresser, and a silver and cut-glass epergne was at the centre of the table, which was set with lace mats and silverware—very plain, with a crest worn by time.

Sarah gave a quick glance around her and sighed with pleasure. Everything in the room was old and perfect and used—not taken for granted, but neither was it hidden away behind cabinet doors or packed in green baize, to be used only on very special occasions.

The food was good too, simple and beautifully cooked, enhanced by the plates upon which it was served; Delft, she recognised, and old, for they were patterned in pale lavender, not the blue one expected. Washing up would be a hazardous undertaking...

She drank the wine she was offered and Mr ter Breukel watched with satisfaction as the colour came back into her pale face. She hadn't been injured but she had been shocked, although she had done her best to hide that. A good night's sleep, he reflected, and tomorrow he would find the time to consider the future.

Suzanne escorted Sarah to her bed, after a cheerful good-night from her host.

Sarah got into the silk and lacy nightie Suzanne had found for her and slid into bed, determined to make sensible plans for the morning; once she had retrieved their luggage and money and passports from the police, she reflected, she could decide what was best to be done. She would have to find out just how long her mother and stepfather would have to stay in hospital… That was as far as she got before falling into a refreshing sleep.

She woke to find Anneke standing by the bed with a little tray of tea and holding her clothes, clean and pressed, over one arm. Anneke beamed at her, nodding in response to her good morning, and handed her a note. The writing was a scrawl; it could have been written by a spider dipped in ink. With difficulty Sarah made out that breakfast was at eight o'clock and she would be taken to the hospital directly after the meal. So she smiled and nodded to Anneke, who smiled and nodded in return, before Sarah drank her tea and got out of bed. There wasn't much time; she showered, dressed, did the best she could with her face and hair, and went downstairs.

Mr ter Breukel and Suzanne were already at the table, but he got up to pull out her chair and expressed the hope that she had slept well.

'Very well,' said Sarah. 'Such a pretty room, and the sort of bed you sink into.'

'Good. You had my note?'

She buttered a roll. 'Yes. What shocking handwriting

you have. But I suppose all medical men write badly so that no one can understand, if you see what I mean?'

Suzanne turned a laugh into a cough, and Mr ter Breukel said gravely, 'I think that is very likely.' He gave her a glance just long enough to take in the delightful sight of her in her cleaned and pressed clothes, no make-up and shining mousy hair. Sarah, not seeing the glance, drank her coffee and remarked that he would be wishing to leave for the hospital and she was quite ready when he wished to go.

'Although I'm sure I should be quite all right to walk to the police station. Unless perhaps I should go to the hospital first?'

'Yes, that would be best. Everything depends on the condition of your mother and stepfather.' He got up from the table. 'You'll excuse me? I must telephone. Could you be ready to leave in ten minutes?'

She got into the car beside him presently; she had bidden Suzanne goodbye and thanked her for her kindness, and Suzanne had kissed her cheek, rather to Sarah's surprise, and said it had been fun. Sarah, thinking about it, supposed that for Suzanne it had been just that, and she had liked her... She liked the man sitting beside her too.

At the hospital he nodded a casual goodbye, said that he would see her later, and handed her over to a nurse who took her to her mother.

Mrs Holt was awake and complaining.

'There you are. I hope you'll arrange for us to go back home as quickly as possible. I shall never recover in this place. Tea with no milk, and nothing but thin bread and butter and a boiled egg.'

Sarah bent to kiss her. 'Did you sleep? Do you feel better this morning?'

'Of course I didn't close my eyes all night, and I feel very poorly. Have you got our things yet? I want my own nightgowns; someone must do my hair...'

'I'm going to collect them this morning; I'll bring whatever you need here, Mother.'

'Have you seen your father?'

'Stepfather,' said Sarah. 'No, Nurse tells me that he is to have his leg seen to this morning.'

'How tiresome.' Mrs Holt turned her head away. 'Go and get my things; when you get back I'll tell you if I want anything else.'

Sarah went through the hospital once more and, because she was a kind girl, asked if she could see her stepfather.

He was in a small ward with three other men, and she saw at a glance that he was in no mood to answer her 'good morning'. She stood listening to his diatribe in reply to her enquiry as to how he felt, and, when he had run out of breath, said that she would come and see him after he had had his operation. Only to be told that he couldn't care less if he never saw her again! So she bade him goodbye and started back to the entrance. Neither parent had asked where she had slept or how she felt.

Getting lost on the way out, she had time to think about her future. She supposed that some time during the day someone at the hospital would tell her how long her mother and stepfather would have to remain there. Mr ter Breukel had told her that someone would arrange their return to England, so it seemed best for her to go back as quickly as possible and look after the house until they returned.

She preferred not to think further ahead than that; life hadn't been easy living at home, her sense of duty outweighing her longing to have a life of her own. But her mother, each time Sarah suggested that she might train for something and be independent, had made life unbearable, with her reproaches and sly reminders that her father had told Sarah to look after her mother. Then, of course, he had had no idea that his wife would remarry—and to a man who was in a position to give her a comfortable life. And who had taken a dislike to his stepdaughter the moment they had met.

She found the main entrance at last, but halfway to it she was stopped.

A porter addressed her in surprisingly good English. She was to wait—he indicated an open doorway beyond which people were sitting.

Perhaps she was to be told what arrangements had been made for her parents. She sat down obediently; there was no point in getting fussed. She had hoped to return to England that day, but probably she would have to spend another night in Arnhem. Which should hold no terrors for her; she would have some money once she had been to the police station, and all she had to do was wait for someone to tell her what to do next.

There were a great many posters on the walls, and she was making futile guesses as to what they were about when the porter tapped her on the shoulder.

She followed him back to the entrance hall and saw Mr ter Breukel standing by the doors. Her smile at the sight of him—filled with relief and delight—shook him badly, but all he said was 'I'll take you to the police station,' with detached courtesy.

CHAPTER TWO

'CAN you spare the time?' asked Sarah anxiously. 'Don't you have patients to see?'

'I have already seen them.' Mr ter Breukel was at his most soothing. 'I shall be operating this afternoon. On your stepfather, amongst others.'

'How soon will I know when he can go home?'

'Probably later this evening. Ah, here is the police station.'

She was glad that he was with her. She gave a succinct account of the accident, and from time to time he was a great help translating some tricky word the officer hadn't understood. All the same it took a long time, and after that the luggage had to be checked, money counted, passports examined. She was given hers, as well as some money from her stepfather's wallet. He wouldn't like that, she reflected, signing for it, but she would need money to get back home. And supposing her mother travelled with her?

She explained that to Mr ter Breukel and waited for his advice.

'Does your mother have traveller's cheques in her handbag?'

The handbag was an expensive one from one of the big fashion houses, unlike Sarah's own rather shabby leather shoulder bag, and there *were* traveller's cheques inside, and quite a lot of money.

'Good. You can give the bag to your mother and she can arrange for it to be kept in safe-keeping until she leaves.'

Put like that, it all sounded very simple. But they went

back to St Bravo's and suddenly nothing was simple any more.

Her mother's X-ray had shown a hairline fracture; there was no question of her leaving the hospital for some time. And there was no time to talk about it, for Mr ter Breukel had been called away the moment they arrived back.

Sarah unpacked what she thought her mother might need, and when that lady demanded her handbag gave it to her. Then she went in search of the ward sister, who told her kindly enough that it would be most unwise for her mother to be moved. 'And, since your father must stay also, they can return together when they are able to travel.'

Sarah went to see the other ward sister about her stepfather then. He was already in Theatre, and Mr ter Breukel was operating. 'Come back later, about six o'clock, and we will tell you what has been done.'

So Sarah went out of the hospital and into the main streets. The luggage was safe with a porter, she had money in her pocket and she was hungry.

She found a small café and sat over coffee and a roll filled with cheese, deciding what she should do next. It made sense to find a tourist information office and find out about getting back home. Maybe not for a few days, but she would need to know...

It wasn't difficult to find, so she went inside and found that the girls behind the counter spoke English. She could fly, they told her, an easy train ride to the airport at Schiphol, or she could get a ferry from the Hoek van Holland or from Scheveningen to Harwich. They could arrange it for her.

Sarah thanked them, then asked if they knew of a small, inexpensive hotel. They went to a lot of trouble, and she left presently with a short list from which to choose. Now it was just a question of going back to St Bravo's, finding out about her stepfather, seeing her mother, collecting her

case from the porter and moving into whichever hotel had
a room vacant.

She went into another café and had a cup of tea and
some biscuits, and then found her way back to the hospital.
She went first to see her stepfather, who was nicely recovered from the anaesthetic but whose temper was uncertain.
He was propped up on his pillows, a leg in plaster under a
cradle. In reply to her civil and sympathetic enquiry as to
how he felt, he said angrily, 'That infernal surgeon says
that I must remain here for at least two weeks...'

'I thought that once the plaster was dry you could walk
with a crutch...'

'Don't be a fool. A broken rib has pierced my lung; it
has to heal before I'm fit to be moved.'

'Oh—oh, I'm sorry. I'll tell Mother. I'm going to see her
now.'

'And don't bother to come and see me. The less I see of
you the better—if it hadn't been for you...'

No doubt he had told anyone who would listen that it
had been her fault. She bade him goodbye and went along
to see her mother.

That lady was sitting up in bed, pecking at her supper.

'It's so early,' she complained, as soon as she set eyes
on Sarah. 'How can I possibly eat at half past six in the
evening?'

Sarah sat down by the bed and listened with outward
patience to her parent's grumbles. When there was a pause,
she told her about her stepfather.

'How tiresome. What is to happen to me, I should like
to know? I've no intention of staying here a day longer
than I must. You will have to take me home, Sarah. Your
father—' she caught Sarah's eye '—stepfather can return
when he's recovered. I can't be expected to look after him.
Of course *you* will be at home, but I suppose you will need
some help.'

She didn't ask Sarah how she had spent her day—Sarah hadn't expected her to—but told her to come the next morning.

'You must get me that special night-cream—and a paler lipstick, oh, and a bed jacket. Pink, something pretty. I don't see why I should look dowdy just because I am in this horrible place.'

'Mother,' said Sarah, 'this is a splendid hospital, and if you hadn't been brought here you might be feeling a lot worse.'

Mrs Holt squeezed out a tear. 'How hard-hearted you are, Sarah. Go away and enjoy yourself—and don't be late here in the morning. I want that bed jacket before the doctors do their rounds.'

Sarah stifled a wish to burst into tears; she was tired and hungry by now, and the future loomed ahead in a most unsatisfactory manner. She bade her mother goodnight and went in search of Sister.

Her mother was doing well, she was told; rather excitable and unco-operative, but that was to be expected with concussion. Sarah could rest assured that hospital was the best place for her mother for the moment, and that as soon as possible she and Mr Holt would be transferred back home.

'So you need have no more worries,' said Sister kindly.

Sarah began the lengthy walk back to the entrance. She must get her case and then go to one of the hotels. She had spent rather longer that she had meant to with her mother, and somewhere a clock chimed seven. She hadn't been looking where she was going and had got lost again. She stood in the long corridor, wondering if she should go to the left or the right...

A hand on her arm swept her straight ahead. 'Lost?' asked Mr ter Breukel cheerfully. 'We'll collect your case and go home. Suzanne will be wondering where we are.'

Sarah, trotting to keep up, and aware that everything was

suddenly all right again, said, 'Well, thank you very much, but I'm going to a hotel. I went to something called VVV and they gave me a list...'

Mr ter Breukel stopped so suddenly that she almost fell over. 'Did I not tell you this morning that you would be staying with us until we know more about your parents? You must forgive me; I have a shocking memory.'

'No, you didn't say anything.' She gave him a thoughtful look. 'You can't have a bad memory; surgeons must have excellent memories, otherwise they would put things back in the wrong place!'

'That is a terrifying thought,' said Mr ter Breukel, grave-faced, and he hurried her along to the entrance. He found a porter to fetch her case, opened his car door, ushered her in and got in beside her.

'The hotel,' said Sarah. 'I mean, I can't impose upon your kindness, really, I can't.'

He said briskly, 'I must tell you about your stepfather, give you some idea of how long he will be with us—and your mother, too. I'm a busy man during the day, so our only chance to discuss this is in the evening. You do agree?'

'Well, yes...'

'Good. Are you hungry?'

'Famished,' said Sarah, without thinking, and then very quickly added, 'I had something to eat in a café.'

'Where?'

'I'm not sure exactly. It said "Snack Bar" over the door.'

'A roll and cheese and a cup of coffee?' He added gently, 'Sarah, you don't need to pretend with me.'

She realised with contented relief that he meant what he said. 'I know that, and I promise I won't do that. I *am* famished.'

Mr ter Breukel's handsome features remained impassive.

A step in the right direction, he reflected. He cast a quick glance at her profile, which she didn't see. Her small nose had a slight tilt to it—most endearing…

What happy chance, reflected Sarah, had led them to meet again like this?

Mr ter Breukel could have told her, of course, but he didn't intend to. He had his own methods of getting information about visitors, and an intimate knowledge of the many corridors of St Bravo's helped.

Suzanne came to meet them as they entered the house. 'Oh, good, you're punctual. Oh, and you've got your case, Sarah. Jaap will take it up to your room, but don't bother to unpack it till later. Come and have a drink before dinner.'

Sarah, rather overwhelmed by this ready welcoming—just as though she had been expected to return, she thought—followed Jaap and her case upstairs and, despite Suzanne's invitation to go straight back down again and have a drink, fished around in her case and found the jersey dress she intended to wear. It was an unpretentious garment, in an inoffensive blue, and she didn't like it much, but it could be rolled up small and stuffed into her case and didn't crease.

She put it on quickly and tidied her hair, did her face rather carelessly and went back downstairs. She would have liked time to make the best of herself—she supposed Mr ter Breukel had that effect on any girl—but she was only here in his house so that he could tell her if any arrangements should be made for her mother and stepfather's return to England…

She accepted a glass of sherry, gave Suzanne an account of her day when she was pressed to do so, glossing over the bits that had been dull, and then ate her dinner, making polite conversation—the weather, the amazing ability of everyone in Arnhem to speak English, the delicious coffee.

Mr ter Breukel listened to her pretty voice, entranced; as

far as he was concerned she could recite the multiplication tables and he would find it exciting. He made suitable replies in a voice of impersonal friendliness, and only as they were drinking their coffee in the drawing room did he begin to tell her about her parents.

They were sitting round the fireplace, she and Suzanne on the vast sofa facing it, he in a great wingback chair with Max lying over his feet. The room looked beautiful, the soft light from the table lamps showing up the magnificent bow-fronted cabinets with their displays of silver and porcelain, casting shadows on the heavy velvet curtains, and yet, despite the magnificence of its contents, the room was welcoming and lived in. And Mr ter Breukel was exactly right for it, thought Sarah; he fitted the room and the room fitted him.

You're letting your imagination run away with you, Sarah told herself silently, and sat up straight because he had put down his coffee cup and saucer and now said briskly, 'Let me tell you what has been done today—your mother is comfortable, but she is, if you will forgive me for saying so, not an easy patient. She wishes to go back to England, naturally enough, but I can't advise that. She needs rest and quiet and to have time to resume her normal outlook on life; I have explained to her that once she is home with your stepfather she will need to feel fit herself.

'I operated on him this afternoon; he has quite a severe fracture of the tibia, which I put together and put in plaster. He will be got up within a few days, but there's no question of him using the leg for weeks. He will be given crutches, but he is a heavy man and not very co-operative. So I think that their return to England must be ruled out for two weeks at least. Arrangements must be made so that they can travel easily, and there must be some kind of nursing aid at your home. Your mother tells me that she would be quite unable to do that. He'll need physiotherapy, and of course the plaster will probably need renewing later on.'

He paused, but Sarah didn't say anything. She was thinking with despair of the weeks ahead, at the beck and call of her stepfather, who would expect her to fulfil the duties of nurse as well as the major tasks of the household. There was a housekeeper, and help for the heavy chores, but there would be the shopping and the ironing and the endless jobs her mother would want done... I mustn't moan, reflected Sarah.

'So I had better go home as quickly as possible and get things arranged.' She thought for a moment. 'I'd have to come back when they're ready to return—to help Mother.'

'That is, of course, one solution.' Mr ter Breukel gave the impression of someone giving friendly advice. 'But I wonder if you have given thought to remaining here and returning with your parents? It so happens that I might be able to offer an alternative solution.

'We have a great-aunt, living in Arnhem, whose companion has had to return to her home to nurse her mother; she may be away for several weeks. You might take over her duties until your parents are ready to leave the hospital. It is probably a job you wouldn't care to undertake—rather dull and needing a good deal of patience. On the other hand, you would have a roof over your head, be able to visit your mother and be here when they are ready to leave.'

'What a splendid idea,' declared Suzanne. She had visited her aunt that very afternoon and her companion, Juffrouw Telle, had been there. Moreover there had been no question of her going home. But Suzanne had no doubt that if Litrik said that Juffrouw Telle was going to nurse her sick mother, then he had contrived something for his own ends. Sarah, thought Suzanne with satisfaction, had done something none of the other women acquaintances in whom he had shown no interest had been able to do—she had stolen his heart.

Suzanne said encouragingly to Sarah, 'Do think about that, Sarah. Great-Aunt is quite an old dear, and you would be able to see your mother every day. I'm sure she would miss you terribly if you went back to England.'

Sarah said, 'Your aunt—great-aunt—might not like me... Besides, her companion might not be ready to return when Mother and my stepfather leave.' She added, 'Or she might come back within the next few days.'

'Unlikely. Her mother will need nursing for ten days at least,' improvised Mr ter Breukel smoothly, 'and if you should have to leave before she returns, then we shall have to find someone else. In the meantime you would be helping several people, and I for one would be most grateful.'

Which reminded Sarah that this was a way in which she could repay him for his kindness. And there was no denying that it was a way out of her problem.

Mr ter Breukel, watching her face, was delighted to see that his plotting and planning were likely to be successful. He reminded himself that he must find a suitable gift for Juffrouw Telle. Middle-aged, patient and kind-hearted, she had been with his great-aunt for years; she was almost one of the family, and had been only too ready to agree to his scheme. It gave her an unexpected holiday, and the pleasure of sharing a secret which held more than a whiff of romance...

Sarah didn't waste time weighing up the pros and cons; the pros were obvious, and if there were any cons she would deal with them later. She said, 'Thank you, I would be glad to help out until your aunt's companion is able to return. And it is I who should be grateful, for now I don't need to worry about anything.'

For the next week or two, at any rate, she added silently. And after that I'll think of something.

Suzanne said, 'Oh, splendid. I'll take you to Great-Aunt tomorrow. In the afternoon? You'll want to see your mother and stepfather first.'

Sarah thanked her, stifling the wish that Mr ter Breukel had offered to take her, reminding herself that he was a busy man and had wasted enough of his time on her anyway.

Her stepfather showed no pleasure at the sight of her, and, apprised of her plans, merely grunted. 'Do what you please, as long as you're back here to look after your mother when we go home. And that can't be soon enough.' He began a tirade against the nurses, the doctors, the food, and the fact that there was no private room available for him. Sarah, having heard it all before, listened patiently and assured him that he would be able to go home the moment he was allowed to, and then she slipped away. It seemed to her that the hospital staff would be only too glad to see the back of him.

Her mother was sitting in the Day Room, reading a magazine, and she greeted Sarah peevishly.

'Should you be reading?' asked Sarah.

'No, but the nurses don't come in here very often, and when they do I hide it under a cushion.' Mrs Holt allowed her mouth to droop. 'I have such a headache.'

'That's because you're reading.'

'Well, I'm bored. I want to go home...'

'I dare say it won't be much longer. Mother, I've got a job. Not paid, of course, but being a companion to an old lady while her usual companion goes home to look after her mother. I may stay there until we go back home.'

'Trust you to find a comfortable place to live while I have to stay in this dreary place.'

Sarah supposed that the concussion had made her mother

so difficult. 'It's not so bad, Mother. I expect I'll be able to come and see you quite often.'

'When you do, bring me some nail varnish. Elizabeth Arden, pink—at least I can give myself a manicure.' Mrs Holt closed her eyes. 'I do have a headache…'

Sarah kissed her and left the hospital. On the way out she caught a glimpse of Mr ter Breukel, enormous even at a distance, surrounded by white-coated satellites. He didn't see her, but the sight of him cheered her up as she walked back to his house.

He had, in fact, turned his head in time to see her disappearing down one of the endless corridors. He would have liked to have taken her himself to his great-aunt's house, but to display too much interest might frighten her off…

Sarah got into Suzanne's car after they had had coffee and was driven into the centre of the city to another old gabled house in a quiet street close to the Grote Kerk. Suzanne didn't give Sarah time to feel nervous. She urged her out of the car, thumped the massive door-knocker and they were admitted before Sarah could draw breath.

The old man who opened the door looked shaky on his legs. He had white hair and pale blue eyes in a wrinkled face. Suzanne threw her arms around him and kissed his cheek, and said something to make him chuckle before she turned to Sarah.

'Kaes has been with Great-Aunt for almost the whole of his life. He's part of the house.' She spoke to him again, and Sarah held out a hand and smiled at the friendly old man. He studied her for a moment and then led them down the hall to double doors on one side of it, opened them, said something to the room's occupant and trotted off.

Suzanne gave Sarah a friendly shove, and Sarah found herself crossing a vast expanse of carpet to the very old lady sitting in a high-backed chair by one of the tall windows.

Suzanne skipped to her side, kissed her and spoke rapidly in Dutch, and then switched to English.

'This is Sarah Beckwith, Tante, come to keep you company until Juffrouw Telle gets back. She can't speak a word of Dutch, but that won't matter, will it? She will be able to read your English novels. You like being read to, don't you?'

The little old lady spoke. She had a soft voice, but now it had a slight edge to it. 'Suzanne, don't mumble. Where is this young woman who is to stay with me until Anna Telle returns? If she mumbles she will be of no use to me.'

Suzanne beckoned Sarah. 'She's here, Tante.'

Sarah stood quietly while she was studied through a pair of lorgnettes, and then took the small be-ringed hand and shook it gently. She said clearly, 'How do you do, *Mevrouw*? I hope I shall be of use to you until Juffrouw Telle returns. I am sorry I can't speak Dutch…'

'No matter, just as long as you speak your own language clearly. Suzanne, ring the bell, Reneke shall take Miss Beckwith to her room. We will have lunch together in half an hour.'

Which meant, reflected Sarah, that she was to go to her room and return in half an hour. She followed a stout, placid woman up the staircase at the end of the hall and into a room at the front of the house. It was large, and the furniture in it was solid. It was comfortable, too, and there were flowers in a little vase on the massive dressing table. There was a bathroom across the passage, as old-fashioned as the room, but equipped with modern comforts. The bath, thought Sarah, eyeing its size, in the middle of the room, balanced on its four iron feet, had been installed for a giant. Her thoughts wandered for a moment; Mr ter Breukel was a giant, and a very nice one…

She unpacked, tidied her person, examined her face in the oval mirror and wished for good looks, applied discreet lipstick and then went to look out of the window. It was tall and wide and gave her an excellent view of the street below and the buildings around it, with the Grote Kerk towering at its end. It was quiet there, but at the other end of the street she could see a busy thoroughfare and the glint of water. She would have to discover the best way to reach the hospital, but just for the moment the hospital, her mother, and all the adherent problems seemed blessedly far away.

She left the window. Like many old houses, this one was peaceful, and people had been happy living in it, just as she had felt at Mr ter Breukel's home.

She wandered round the room, looking at the few pictures on its wall, picking up ornaments and putting them down again. She hoped that she would see Mr ter Breukel again, for she liked him. She examined a small porcelain figure on the bedside table, a charming trifle probably worth a small fortune. She was thinking too much about him and that wouldn't do. He had been kind, but he was a man to be kind—to an old woman crossing the street, or to a lost dog. Probably he would forget all about her now that she was dealt with—a problem solved...

The half-hour was up; she went back to the room where the old lady and Suzanne were waiting.

'After lunch, when Suzanne has gone, I will explain your duties to you,' said her hostess. 'They are, I believe, not onerous. You will be able to visit your mother at St Bravo's. I am sure that we shall get on well together.'

They had their lunch in a sombre room panelled in some dark wood, sitting at a table which would seat ten perfectly comfortably. It was a simple meal, beautifully served, and Sarah, who had been dreading it, found that she was enjoying herself. Old Mevrouw ter Breukel might be getting on in years, but there was nothing wrong with her brain. She was as sharp as a needle: up to date with politics, fashion and the latest books.

Presently wishing Suzanne goodbye, Sarah assured her that she was going to be happy in her unexpected job. 'I'll do my best to please your aunt,' she said. 'You've been so kind, and so has Mr ter Breukel. Thank you both very much. I'll let you know when I'm going back to England.'

'Do, though I'll probably see you before then. I hope you won't find it too dull.'

Sarah thought of the uneventful life she led at home. 'It's the most exciting thing that's happened to me in years.'

Her duties were indeed light: she was to spend a good deal of the day with Mevrouw ter Breukel, reading, writing letters for her, fetching and carrying such odds and ends as the lady wanted, and making sure that she was comfortable and lacked for nothing. In the afternoon she was to have an hour or so free, and there would be plenty of time to go and see her mother.

Once her duties had been made known to her she was bidden to fetch a book and read aloud until the old lady had her afternoon nap.

The book took Sarah by surprise. It was the latest Ruth Rendell.

'Juffrouw Telle doesn't read English well, and it tires me to read. We will read as many books as possible while you are here,' said Mevrouw ter Breukel surprisingly. 'Litrik keeps me supplied with the books I enjoy—Jack Higgins, P.D. James, Evelyn Anthony, Freeling. Sit there, child, I hear better on this side. I'm halfway through the book— there's a bookmark.'

Sarah found the place and started to read. She had a pleasant voice and the story was exciting; it kept them both absorbed until an elderly woman brought in the tea tray.

'No milk, no sugar,' commanded the old lady, 'and I'll have a biscuit.'

Sarah drank her tea from a paper-thin cup and answered the questions which Mevrouw ter Breukel fired at her in a soft voice. No, she didn't have a young man, nor had she any prospect of marrying one, and, no, she didn't have a job. Her life, outlined for the old lady's benefit, sounded dull in her ears.

They dined later, the two of them, in the dark grandeur of the dining room, and Sarah was glad that she had changed into the blue jersey, for Mevrouw ter Breukel was wearing black taffeta and diamonds.

Told, kindly enough, to go to bed soon after the *stoel* clock struck ten, Sarah went willingly. She wasn't tired, but the old lady had observed that occasionally, when she was unable to sleep, she expected someone to keep her company during the wakeful hours. But nothing happened to disturb Sarah's sleep.

She was up and dressed by eight o'clock and had gone, as she had been told, to Mevrouw ter Breukel's room, to find that old lady sitting up in a vast bed, a four-poster, doing a jigsaw puzzle.

They exchanged good mornings and Sarah spent five minutes picking up bits of the puzzle which had been flung aside before she was told to go and have her breakfast.

'And bring me my letters in half an hour or so. Then I shall not need you for a hour or more. Go to the hospital, if you wish, and enquire about your parents. Kaes will look after you and tell you how to get to St Bravo's.'

Dismissed, Sarah went downstairs and found Kaes waiting for her. Her breakfast had been laid with great elegance in a small room behind the dining room, and she enjoyed every morsel of it, keeping an eye on the clock. Half an hour later she went back with the post, and found Mevrouw ter Breukel still engrossed in her puzzle.

'Run along now, and be back here by half past ten.'

The hospital was ten minutes' walk away, and there were several ambulances parked by the Accident Room entrance. She went up to her mother's ward and met Sister coming out of the office.

'You have come to see your mother? She has slept well; she will be glad to see you. We are busy today. There has been a multiple car accident, and soon we shall have more patients here.'

Mrs Holt was sitting by a window. 'You must do some shopping for me,' she began, without preamble. 'I need some more mascara and another lipstick, and see if you can get me a decent magazine; I've nothing to read…'

'Don't they come round with books? I'm sure they'd find you something in English, Mother.'

'Oh, yes, but you know how quickly reading bores me.'

'TV?'

'In Dutch, my dear? You must be joking. I'm to see the consultant this morning. I shall ask to go home.'

'What about my stepfather?'

'Oh, they will arrange to send him home, too, of course. He must be able to travel by now.'

'Have you been to see him?'

'My dear Sarah, I'm not well; my nerves wouldn't stand it. Sister tells me from time to time how he is. You had better go and see him.'

Sarah went, unwillingly enough, but she saw it as her duty. It was a waste of time, of course. Her stepfather did not wish to see her. Her visit was brief and she soon made her way back to the entrance, hoping that she might meet Mr ter Breukel; he would be too busy to stop and talk, but it would be nice just to say hello.

They met on a staircase. She was going down as he was going up, two steps at a time, followed by two younger men in long white coats. He didn't pause; she doubted if he had seen her.

He had, of course, but sudden emergencies took no account of personal feelings.

Sarah had the good sense to see that she had probably been invisible to him; he was so obviously involved in some dire situation. He had looked different, too, and she realised why. He had been wearing grey trousers and a high-necked pullover, and he hadn't shaved. Perhaps he had been up half the night.

The whole night, actually.

There was no time to shop for her mother, and she hurried back to Mevrouw ter Breukel, anxious not to be late.

The day went smoothly and pleasantly enough, and, to her surprise, quickly. She was kept busy, and when the old lady discovered that she could play chess, after a fashion, the evening hours were fully occupied. Sarah went to bed at length, feeling that the day had gone well. Only it would have been nice if Mr ter Breukel had called to see his aunt.

A wish, had she but known it, which he would have heartily endorsed.

But he came the next day. It was the quiet hour or so after tea, and Sarah was setting out the chess pieces, ready for a game after dinner, her neat head bent over the chessboard. He stood in the open doorway, watching her, studying her small person, wanting very much to go to her and gather her into his arms and tell her that he loved her. But not just yet, he warned himself, and went into the room.

His great-aunt was clearly taking a nap. Sarah turned round and saw him and smiled and put her finger to her lips. He smiled back, took her arm and led her to the far end of the room by the window. Only then did he say, 'Hello, Sarah.'

She beamed up at him. 'Hello. Mevrouw ter Breukel will wake presently. Do you want tea or anything?'

'Nothing, thank you. Have you settled down? Not too hard work?'

'I'm very happy, and it isn't like work at all. Your great-aunt is a darling old lady.' She spoke in a whisper, and, when he didn't answer, asked, 'Have you been busy? There were a lot of ambulances when I went to see Mother yesterday.'

'A day of emergencies.'

'I—I saw you yesterday—you didn't see me. It was on the stairs. You looked as though you have been up all night.'

'It was a night of emergencies, too. Sarah, before you return to England, I should like to show you something of Holland. I shall be free on Sunday, will you spend it with me?'

'With you? You mean all day?' The delight in her face changed to regret. 'But I can't; I'm here to be your aunt's companion.'

'But like all companions you are entitled to a free day each week. Besides, Suzanne is coming to spend the day here, and you won't be needed.'

When she would have protested, he added casually, 'I think we might enjoy each other's company.'

'Yes, well—but there must be other people—I mean friends you'd rather be with.'

'They are always here. You will go home shortly, and I think that you deserve at least a brief glimpse of Holland!'

'Well, thank you. I would like it very much.' And, Sarah being Sarah, she added, 'I'm afraid I'm not a very interesting person to be with. I mean, I'm not clever or witty. You might get bored...'

Mr ter Breukel's expression of calm interest didn't alter. 'After the rush and hurry of St Bravo's I dare say I shall find your company restful. Shall we say nine o'clock on Sunday morning?'

'All right. But I must ask Mevrouw ter Breukel's permission.'

She was interrupted by that lady's voice demanding to know what they were talking about, and when she was told she observed that it suited her very well. 'For if Suzanne is to spend the day with me I'll not need Sarah here as well. Take her through the Veluwe, Litrik, and show her how lovely it is there.'

She offered a cheek for his kiss. 'Sarah, go for a walk, or amuse yourself for half an hour or so. We will have our game of chess after dinner.'

When Sarah had gone, and he had shut the door behind her, she said, 'Litrik, I may be an old woman but I still have my wits about me. You're in love with the girl, aren't you?'

He came and sat down opposite to her, speaking Dutch now. 'Yes, my dear. I knew that the moment I set eyes on her.'

'But she has no idea of that. Only she likes you very much indeed, I think.'

'Perhaps I am too old for her.'

'That's not going to stop you...'

Mr ter Breukel laughed. 'No, it's not!'

CHAPTER THREE

SARAH woke on Sunday to a fine spring morning. True, the sky was a very pale blue and held no warmth, but the tiled roofs of the houses around her sparkled and the air, when she leaned out of the window, was fresh.

At nine o'clock precisely she was borne away in the discreet luxury of Mr ter Breukel's Rolls, unaware of her companion's delight at her company since he had greeted her with casual friendliness and now began almost immediately to describe the various parts of Arnhem as he drove out of the city: the war memorial at the Rhine Bridge, the parks, the old houses which had survived the destruction of the War, the zoo.

Sarah craned her neck from side to side, anxious not to miss anything.

He drove north presently, through the High Veluwe national park, taking the narrow by-roads through the woods and stopping for coffee in Apeldoorn, where he walked her to the palace of Het Loo.

The park was open and they wandered to and fro, explored the stable block, which was open to the public, and then got back into the car to drive on to Zwolle. Here they lunched at a small restaurant housed in an ancient house by the Stads Gracht, once a moat and now a canal, and were served *koffietafel*—a basket of various rolls and bread and slices of cheese on a vast platter, cold meat and sausage, hard-boiled eggs and a salad, accompanied by a pot of coffee.

Sarah eyed the table with pleasure; the morning's sightseeing and her pleasure in her companion's company had given her an appetite, moreover she felt happy. Somehow in Mr ter Breukel's placid company the future became vague and unthreatening.

They travelled on presently, through Meppel and into Friesland, to stop for tea in Sneek, and then had a brief glimpse of the lake before driving on to the coast. It was chilly here, and the North Sea looked grey and forbidding.

'Lovely in the summer,' Mr ter Breukel told her. 'Those islands you can see are popular with families. There are splendid beaches for children. You like children?'

Sarah was unaware of how wistful she looked. 'Oh, yes…'

Children, she thought, and dogs and cats and a donkey, and an old house with a huge garden—and a husband, of course. And what chance had she of getting any of them? The future, so pleasantly vague, suddenly became only too real.

Mr ter Breukel took her arm and walked her back to the car. In some way his hand on hers dispelled her gloomy thoughts. The future didn't matter, not for the moment at any rate.

He drove back over the Afsluitdijk, gave her a glimpse of Alkmaar and raced south, bypassing Amsterdam. 'You shall see that another time,' he told her casually. 'There's rather a nice place where we can have dinner just outside Utrecht.'

The 'nice place' was a seventeenth-century mansion, very splendid, overlooking a pond and tucked away in the centre of a small wood. Sarah, led away to a well-equipped cloakroom, did her hair and face, wishing for chestnut curls and a pretty face as she did so, wishing too that she was wearing a smart outfit worthy of her companion and her surroundings. She told herself in her sensible way not to be silly, and joined Mr ter Breukel in a large, rather old-fashioned lounge to sip her sherry while they discussed what they should eat.

Sarah, with gentle prompting from Mr ter Breukel, chose tiny pancakes filled with goat's cheese, sole served with a champagne sauce, and chocolate and almond pudding. She ate with a splendid appetite, her tongue nicely loosened by the white wine he had chosen, so that by seemingly casual questions he was made the recipient of a good deal of information concerning her life at Clapham Common. Not that she complained about it; it was what she *didn't* say that gave him an insight into its dullness. He was impatient to rescue her at once, but that, of course, was impossible. He must rely on a kindly Fate and his own plans.

Sarah looked up and caught his eye and smiled, and he schooled his features into a friendly glance and made a casual remark about their surroundings. He wondered what the surrounding diners would do if he were to swoop across the table and pick Sarah up and carry her off. Somewhere quiet, where he could kiss her at leisure. He smiled then, and Sarah said, 'Oh, it's lovely here. I shall remember it all when I get back home.'

'Good. You have only seen a small part of Holland, though.'

And all she was likely to see, thought Sarah. He hadn't suggested that he would take her out again, and she hadn't expected him to. But supposing he thought that she had hoped he *would*. She had done her best to be good company, but probably he had found her rather dull, and after all he had been more than kind.

Suzanne was still at the house when they got back.

'I've helped Great-Aunt to bed,' she told them. 'We've had a lovely day, gossiping and playing backgammon. Did you two enjoy yourselves?'

Her brother said gravely that for his part he had had a

most interesting day, which Sarah considered was neither one thing or the other.

'It was lovely,' she told Suzanne. 'I'll have so much to remember when I get back home.'

She bade them goodnight presently, before they drove away, and then went to her room and went to bed, remembering every minute of the day. Mr ter Breukel hadn't said anything about seeing her again, but of course they were bound to meet, even if it were only to make arrangements for her mother and stepfather's return to England. Besides, she reminded herself, he visited his great-aunt frequently.

But there was no sign of him. She had caught the occasional glimpse of him in the distance when she had visited her mother at the hospital, but he'd been so far away that only the size and height of him had made her sure that it was he. Certainly he didn't visit his great-aunt again, nor were there any messages concerning the transfer to England of her mother.

Mrs Holt, while still complaining bitterly, had settled down at last to the quiet routine of the hospital, and Sister had assured Sarah that she should be fit to return home very shortly. And her stepfather, although one of the worst patients the ward sister assured Sarah that she had ever had to nurse, was fit to travel.

'You will be told when arrangements have been made,' she said to Sarah kindly.

The best part of a week went by; there was no news of Juffrouw Telle's return, and when Sarah saw Suzanne, which was frequently, that young lady professed to know nothing.

It was on an early morning, when Sarah went down to her breakfast after peeping in to see if the old lady was still sleeping, that she found Mr ter Breukel sitting at the table in the small room where she took her meals when she was alone. Everything necessary for a good breakfast was arranged around him, and a folded newspaper was beside his plate.

Sarah paused in the doorway, delighted to see him but not sure if she was welcome. She said, 'Hello,' and then, more sedately, 'Good morning, Mr ter Breukel.'

He had got to his feet and pulled out a chair, and she saw that he was wearing a grey sweater and corduroy trousers. 'You've been up all night,' she observed, and indeed he looked tired; he had showered, but there were lines in his face which she hadn't seen before. 'I hope you will go straight to bed when you've had your breakfast.'

Mr ter Breukel, who had other plans, said that yes, he would, in a meek voice, and pushed the coffee pot towards her.

Sarah said in her practical way, 'Shouldn't you be at your own home?'

He had forgotten how tired he was; he looked into the future and saw with deep satisfaction homecomings in the small hours to Sarah's wifely concern.

'Indeed I should, but it seemed a good opportunity to see you about your mother and stepfather's transfer to England. It has been arranged for Tuesday—that gives you three days to carry out any plans you may have made. Your stepfather will need to travel by ambulance, and your mother can go with him. You will fly from Schiphol and an ambulance will collect you at Heathrow and get you home to Clapham. You will be travelling with them, of course. Someone will come for you on Tuesday morning at eight o'clock.'

Sarah didn't speak for a bit; she was battling with the sudden fright that she wasn't going to see him again. She choked it down and said gruffly, 'Thank you for making all the arrangements; we're very much in your debt. We're very grateful.' Well, *she* was; she wasn't sure about her

mother and stepfather. 'I'll be ready, and if there's anything
I should do, will someone let me know? And what about
your great-aunt? I've loved being with her, and she does
need someone, you know...'

Mr ter Breukel buttered a roll lavishly. 'It is amazing
how things arrange themselves,' he observed blandly.
'Juffrouw Telle phoned last night to say that she would be
returning on Monday evening.'

'Her mother's better? I'm glad, and how provi...'

'...dential,' finished Mr ter Breukel. 'Great-Aunt has enjoyed your company and you have been a great help to us.
I'm only sorry you haven't had more time to see Holland.'

'I had a lovely day with you,' said Sarah. 'I shall remember it always.' She added hastily, in case he thought
she meant him and his company, 'The country was delightful.'

He kept a straight face while he watched the colour wash
over her cheeks. To have accompanied her to England
would have been a delight, but he had decided against. First
let her return to her own home; there was always the possibility that, viewed from the other side of the North Sea,
their growing friendship might dwindle into a vague interlude. That was something he would have to discover later.

He smiled gently. 'Yes, it was a delightful day.' And
five minutes later he was leaving, with the casual remark
that he would see her before she left Arnhem.

'And go to bed—just for an hour or two,' said Sarah, in
such a concerned voice that he was tempted to pick her up
and kiss her. But he didn't, and bed, as far as he could see,
was something to be deferred until he had dealt with his
patients. So he smiled, patted her on a shoulder and was
gone.

Sarah, visiting her mother later that day, found her in a
state of excitement and with numerous requests to Sarah
which she hadn't a hope of fulfilling. She pointed out that

once they were home her mother could buy the things she declared she must have, that there was no need to be made up, have her hair done or send Sarah to buy the host of small unnecessary articles she required.

'Of course you *would* say that,' declared Mrs Holt crossly. 'The smallest thing I ask you to do for me and you have a reason for not doing it.'

She turned a shoulder to Sarah. 'You had better go and see your stepfather and see if he needs anything. And you're not to leave me on the journey. I feel ill at the very thought of it.'

Come to think of it, thought Sarah, I feel ill too...

Her stepfather did nothing to improve matters; he queried and argued about every arrangement made for his transfer, and grumbled that his car, which had been transported back to Clapham, was no doubt damaged beyond repair and that no one had seen fit to give him any information about it. He grumbled, too, at the expense of the ambulance, the special arrangements which had been made at the airports—indeed there was nothing about which he *didn't* grumble!

And Sarah made it worse by asking him for money to buy a thank-you gift for the nursing staff. She waited stoically while he vented his rage at the very idea, and then said, 'I should think about a hundred *gulden* would do—for a really handsome box of chocolates they can share around.'

There was no sign of Mr ter Breukel on Tuesday morning; her farewells said, Sarah was driven away to the hospital and found the ambulance already there. Her stepfather was already in it; she could hear his irate voice complaining bitterly about something—a useless exercise as everyone there was occupied with getting Mrs Holt into the ambulance in her turn. Now that she was actually leaving she had become a bundle of doubts, and it was only when Sarah arrived that she would consent to get into the ambulance.

Sarah went round the small group of nurses and the two ward sisters, uttering thanks and offering the chocolates. They must be glad to see the back of us, she reflected, dragging out her goodbyes for as long as possible, just in case Mr ter Breukel should come.

There was no reason why he should; Suzanne had wished her goodbye on the previous evening, and they had parted with mutual regret that their friendship would have to end. She would have liked to have said goodbye to Mr ter Breukel, too, although she didn't think that *he* would feel any regret...

She couldn't spin the time out any longer, and went round to the front of the ambulance; she was to sit with the driver so that the paramedic with him could travel with her mother and stepfather. She reached up to open the door, and Mr ter Breukel's large hand lifted her hand away and opened it for her.

'Have a safe journey,' he told her. 'Make sure that you get all the documents before you board the plane, the driver will let you have them at Schiphol. I've written to your doctor, of course, and sent the X-rays to him; if he needs to know anything further he can reach me here.'

Sarah nodded. Now that she was actually seeing him for the last time she could think of nothing to say. If only she could think of something which would remind him of her— she frowned fiercely at the ridiculous idea and offered a hand. She said, 'Thank you for all that you have done. Everyone has been so kind and we must have been a nuisance...'

He didn't deny that, but said, 'You have been happy here, despite the circumstances?'

'Yes, oh, yes.'

He smiled then, still holding her hand, and then gave it

back to her and opened the door. Sarah whispered, 'Good-bye,' and got in, because there was nothing else that she could do. She could have got out again, of course, and refused to go, causing confusion and embarrassment to everyone there. For one wild moment she considered this, but only for a moment. She smiled and waved and was driven away, back to Clapham.

The journey went smoothly, despite untold hold-ups and complaints from the Holts, and they arrived in the late afternoon to find Mrs Twist, the housekeeper, waiting for them.

This was by far the hardest part of the journey for Sarah. She had coped well enough with documents, passports, various officials, her mother's endless demands and her stepfather's rantings, but now, once more in their own house, they both demanded instant attention.

Her mother wished to be put to bed immediately, and cosseted with a light meal, the male nurse who had been engaged to attend to Mr Holt hadn't arrived, and although Mr Holt was quite able to do a good deal for himself he also demanded assistance, and Mrs Twist, good soul though she was, found it all a bit too much and retired to the kitchen in tears.

It was long past midnight by the time the house was at last quiet and Sarah could take herself off to bed. The nurse hadn't turned up. It was to be hoped that he would arrive in the morning...

Dr Benson came first. Mrs Twist and Sarah had just finished dealing with breakfast, and Sarah, who had known him for some years, welcomed him with open arms, handed over the various letters and papers she had been given and then went to admit the nurse. He was a sober, middle-aged man, who looked capable of dealing with her stepfather's ill temper. He would come each day, he told her, for a couple of hours in the morning and again in the early evening.

Which left a good deal of the day during which Mr Holt would expect attention. But now that her mother was well again she could perhaps be persuaded to spend an hour or two with him each afternoon, thought Sarah hopefully.

They settled down to an uneasy routine, for Mrs Holt couldn't be relied upon to keep to any routine, and was liable to go off for an afternoon's shopping in a taxi without warning anyone, returning exhausted and demanding Sarah's instant attention.

It was on Dr Benson's third visit that he brought his partner with him: Robert Swift, a young man with a cheerful face and a friendly way with him.

Over a cup of coffee, after visiting his patient, he told Sarah that he intended to stay in Clapham. 'I've got rooms here,' he told her, 'but I'm getting married next year and we've got our eyes on a rather nice flat close to the Common. We're both Londoners and Jennie likes it here. I'm jolly lucky to be taken on as Dr Benson's partner.'

Sarah liked him and listened, whenever he called, to his hopes for the future while he drank the coffee she always had ready for him.

They had been back a week when he suggested that she might like to go with him to see the flat he hoped to buy. 'I told Jennie about you,' he told her ingenuously. 'She's gone up to Yorkshire to nurse an aunt. You've lived here for a few years, haven't you, so you would know if it's in a decent part of Clapham. We want somewhere nice; I don't want Jennie to work when we're married.'

'I'd love to come. It would have to be when Kenneth's here—but the morning's no good for you, is it? He comes back each afternoon about five o'clock and stays for two hours.'

'Suits me! How about tomorrow? It's my half-day.' He

gave her a friendly look. 'You don't get much time to your-self, do you?'

'Not just at the moment, but my stepfather is to have crutches very soon, and that will be a lot easier.'

A statement not to be believed for one moment. Mr Holt on crutches would be a menace, going round the house, interfering with all and sundry. Now, more or less chained to his bed, he had to be content to supervise his business by telephone, and an occasional visit from one of his un-derlings, but once up and about there would be no holding him. He wouldn't be able to drive the new car which had replaced the damaged one, which meant that Sarah would be expected to chauffeur him if he took a fancy to go to the office. And that would annoy her mother, who regarded her as an unpaid companion.

She must escape, but how?

Robert Swift arrived punctually the next day, and since Kenneth was already in the house Sarah went away to put on her outdoor things, find her mother and explain that she would be back within the hour. Robert was waiting in the hall and they went to the door together. It was a rather hideous door, with coloured glass panels and a loud bell. Somebody was ringing it now; she opened the door, laugh-ing at something Robert had said as she did so.

Mr ter Breukel stood there.

'Oh, it's you,' cried Sarah. 'Oh, I never expected…!' Delight at the sight of him had taken her breath.

Mr ter Breukel said, in a calm voice which allowed none of his feelings to show, 'Hello, Sarah. I'm over here for a short while and thought I would look you up, but I see I've called at an awkward time. Don't let me keep you.'

'You're not—that is, we're only going to look at a flat. This is Dr Swift.' She looked at Robert. 'Mr ter Breukel is

a consultant surgeon at the hospital where my stepfather
and mother were…'

Mr ter Breukel offered a hand. 'They're doing well, I
hope?'

'Yes—I'm only Dr Benson's junior partner, sir. Did you
wish to see them? I'm sure Dr Benson…'

'No, no. I'll be phoning him before I go back to Holland.
I'm sure they are in excellent hands.'

He smiled down at Sarah. 'I'm glad to see you looking
so well and happy, Sarah. Suzanne sent her love.'

'She did? You'll come and see us before you go?'

He said smoothly, 'I doubt if I'll have the time. And I
mustn't keep you from viewing this flat.' He looked at
Robert. 'You intend to settle here?'

'Oh, yes. We both know this part of London well, and
it's a splendid practice.'

Mr ter Breukel offered a hand again. 'Then I must wish
you a happy future. And you too, of course, Sarah.' He
smiled. 'It didn't take you long to discover that Clapham
has its advantages over Arnhem.'

His handshake was brief, and she was still gathering her
woolly wits together when he turned, walked down the
short drive, got into his car and drove away.

'He seems a nice chap,' said Robert. 'Not so young, of
course. But good at his job, I dare say.'

Sarah swallowed the tears which had kept her silent.
'He's very nice, and he's quite young and very clever. Shall
we go? I mustn't be away for too long.'

Robert was too full of his own plans to notice her silence.
She admired the flat, agreed that it was in a good neighbourhood and would make a perfect home for his Jennie,
and presently he drove her back.

'I won't ask you in,' she told him at the door. 'Mother
expects me to see to her supper and help get her ready for
bed.'

'Of course. But surely Mrs Holt feels quite fit again?'

'Well, yes, Dr Benson says she's very well, but she— she suffers from her nerves and likes someone to—to be with her...'

Robert gave her a thoughtful look. 'A companion sounds the right answer to that. Wouldn't you like to be independent—find a job?'

'Very much, but it's not very easy at the moment. Perhaps when my stepfather is quite recovered.' She added, in a bitter little voice, 'But, you see, I'm not trained for anything.'

'There are dozens of things you could do—a few months' training at whatever you choose and you're on your way.'

'You're right, Robert, and I'll see what I can do about it. You must think me a very spineless person.'

'No, you're a dutiful daughter tied by the leg.' He grinned suddenly. 'You have nice legs too. Goodbye, Sarah, I'll be in some time tomorrow.'

Sarah managed not to think too much about Mr ter Breukel that evening, but later, in bed, lying awake thinking about him, going over their brief meeting word for word, she was quite suddenly struck by an appalling thought, He had asked about Robert's flat, but Robert hadn't mentioned his Jennie, and then Mr ter Breukel had wished them both a happy future, and that would explain his remark about her liking Clapham better than Arnhem.

He thought that she and Robert were going to marry. What must he think of her after she had told him so plainly that she had no plans to marry, no boyfriend, and had let him see that she liked him?

And she had no idea where he was; she couldn't write and explain, let alone go and see him. He was in London, she supposed, but London was vast... She told herself to be sensible, and to think sensibly too. Presently she got out of bed and searched through her handbag. Sure enough, Suzanne had written down her phone number. 'So that we can give each other a ring from time to time,' she had said. And I will, decided Sarah, as soon as possible in the morning.

She got back into bed, and presently cried herself to sleep.

Breakfast dealt with, she went to her stepfather's study and dialled Suzanne's number. 'It's me,' she said in answer to a sleepy hello. 'Sarah. Mr ter...that is, your brother came to see us yesterday, only I was just going out and I—I wanted to see him but he went away and I don't know where he is. If I did I could go and see him or phone him...'

She wasn't being very sensible; Suzanne must think she was being silly.

Suzanne, who had known that Litrik was going to England, added two and two together and made five before Sarah could speak again.

'He's in London for several days. I'll give you his number and his address, and he'll be at two or three hospitals. Wait while I get my pocketbook.'

She read out the numbers, added addresses and advised Sarah to go and see him. 'You know how it is if you phone. Some dragon tells you he isn't there or he's engaged with a patient. That first address I gave you is the most likely—he'll be seeing private patients there in the mornings between nine o'clock and noon while he's in London. Nice to hear from you, Sarah.'

Her mother didn't take kindly to the idea of Sarah going off at a moment's notice that morning, but Sarah went all the same. She hadn't enough money for a taxi, and anyway her mother would want to know exactly why she needed to go somewhere in such a hurry, but the rush hour was over and a bus shouldn't take too long. However, she had reckoned without an unkind Fate; an accident held up the traffic, buses were diverted... She reached the hospital at five minutes to twelve, and by the time she had asked her way to the wing used for consulting rooms it was five past the hour. And Mr ter Breukel, she was told, had been gone for five minutes.

'You don't know where?' asked Sarah of the receptionist.

The girl unwrapped a chocolate bar and took a bite. 'No idea. He won't be here in the hospital again today. You're not a patient?'

Sarah shook her head. 'No—I—it doesn't matter.'

So she went back home and, being a girl who liked to finish what she had started, studied the phone numbers and addresses Suzanne had given her. She decided against ringing him up—either one talked too much or too little on the phone—but there was a likely address. She looked it up on the street map in her stepfather's study and decided that it must be a private house, close to Harley Street. Either he would have rooms there or it was a service flat. If he was working he would hardly be at a hotel.

Her mind made up, she helped Mrs Twist with lunch, spent the afternoon with her mother, had tea with her and took tea to her stepfather, then went to the kitchen to help Mrs Twist with dinner.

The evening would be the best time to go and see Mr ter Breukel, she had decided, and to strike while the iron was hot seemed good sense. Kenneth had arrived, and would be with her stepfather for a couple of hours, and friends had called to see her mother.

'I'm going out,' she told Mrs Twist. 'I don't expect I'll be very long. I'll tell Mother before I go, but don't fuss if I'm not back in time for dinner.'

It was a chilly evening, but light, so she put on a coat

over her jersey dress, did her face and hair carefully, told her mother that she would be back presently and set out once more. It was quite a long journey and she had ample time to rehearse what she wanted to say. She wouldn't stay, of course—after a day's work he would be tired—but she had to explain...

The address she had been given was one of a row of rather grand houses with steps leading up to their important front doors. Not the kind of house one would have expected to have been turned into flats. The curtains were drawn across the windows but there was a light showing through the transom above the door. She glanced at her watch; it was almost eight o'clock—later than she had thought, but it was too late to turn back now. She thumped the great brass knocker.

The door was opened by a severe-looking maid, very correctly dressed in a black dress with a white apron.

'Mr ter Breukel?' asked Sarah. 'He is staying here, I believe?'

'Yes, miss.' The girl wasn't unfriendly and Sarah took heart.

'Could I see him for a few minutes? If you would take my name...'

The girl stood aside and Sarah passed her into an elegant hall. 'Who shall I say, miss?'

'Sarah Beckwith—Miss.' She followed the girl across the hall and was close behind her when she opened one of the doors. The room, large, splendidly furnished and brilliantly lighted, was full of people dressed for the evening, drinks in their hands, and right at the end of it she could see Mr ter Breukel, elegant in black tie, talking to a group of equally elegant men and women.

The maid had left her, and Sarah, good sense flown out of her head, stood where she was, rooted to the spot. This was something she hadn't even imagined. She saw the maid speak to Mr ter Breukel and he looked up and saw her. He was a good way off, but near enough for her to see that he wasn't smiling. A belated idea to get out of the house as quickly as possible was nipped in the bud, because now he had spoken to a man nearby and was crossing the room.

'Oh, dear,' said Sarah and backed away. She would apologise for disturbing his evening and leave smartly…

His 'Good evening, Sarah,' was uttered in a voice which told her nothing, and after she asked the maid where they might go she followed him meekly across the hall and into a small room, cosily furnished and rather untidy. There was a large ginger cat curled up before the small fire, who took no notice of them as they went in.

'Do sit down,' said Mr ter Breukel. 'You wanted to see me urgently? Your parents?'

Sarah sat down on a small easy chair and the cat jumped onto her lap and was instantly asleep. She took one or two deep breaths, because she had read somewhere that that was the way to calm one's nerves.

'I'm sorry, I didn't know that you would be having a party. I tried to see you at the hospital this morning, but you had gone. There was a hold-up and the bus had to make a detour—the passengers got very annoyed, but really it wasn't the driver's fault…' She stopped, aware that she wasn't getting to the point, and Mr ter Breukel, watching her, fell in love with her all over again.

He said gently, 'You wanted to see me?'

She gave him a grateful glance. 'Yes, about yesterday. If I'd have known that you would be coming to see us, I would have told Robert not to come.'

'A wise decision…'

'Yes, well, you see, I could go and see the flat at any time—that is, when he's free—but you were unexpected, and anyway I didn't think fast enough. I should have told Robert to go away.'

'He seems a very pleasant young man. Only a little older than yourself?'

'He's thirty. I'm twenty-three. But you know that. What I wanted to make quite clear....' Her thoughts, darting here and there like mice in a trap, had taken on a life of their own. 'Do you live here? Suzanne gave me this address. It's a very nice house.'

Mr ter Breukel said with careful nonchalance, 'She phones you from time to time, I expect? She likes you.'

'I like her, too; she's so pretty. No, I phoned her. You see, I wanted to see you and make things clear.'

He crossed one leg over the other. Presumably his Sarah would soon come to the point. She was behaving as though she felt guilty about this Robert. He felt a dull despair at the thought of her marrying him, but if she was going to be happy then he would learn to live without her. He had allowed himself to daydream; he should have known better at his age. What girl would want to marry a man twelve years older than she?

Somewhere in the house a gong sounded, and Sarah said, 'Oh, dear, that's for dinner. You must go.'

'We haven't got very far, have we?' he said, and his voice was kind. 'You have been trying to tell me that you're going to marry Robert and for some reason you're scared to do so. I'm delighted for you, Sarah, and I'm sure you will be very happy.'

The door opened behind them and a young woman poked her head round it.

'Forgive me, but we're just going in to dinner. Perhaps your friend would like to stay?'

Sarah had got to her feet. 'No, no. I was just going. I'm sorry to have interrupted.'

She smiled at the young woman, who smiled back and disappeared down the hall. 'Come when you are ready, Litrik,' she called over a shoulder.

The maid was in the hall, waiting to open the door. Sarah made for it in a rush. To get out of the house and away from Mr ter Breukel was vital, for once out in the street she could cry as much as she wanted. She had made a fine mess of everything, but perhaps that was a good thing for he had said that he was delighted that she would be marrying Robert.

She put out a hand and had it shaken gently, muttered something, she had no idea what, and left the house very nearly at a run. If he had said anything to her she hadn't heard him, but really there was nothing more to say, was there? She began to walk very fast, letting the buses pass her. She had been a fool; all her carefully rehearsed speeches had been forgotten and she had talked a lot of rubbish—and anyway, what did it matter to him if she married someone else? Why had she been so anxious to explain his mistake in thinking that?

She gave a great gulping sob. She wasn't going to get married anyway. 'And I dare say I never shall,' she said, and a passer-by gave her a wary look.

She caught a bus presently, and went home to face Mrs Twist's anxious face, her mother's complaining voice and her stepfather roaring from his room.

'Not one of my best days,' said Sarah to herself later, gobbling her warmed-up dinner at the kitchen table. Mrs Twist had gone to bed, and presently she would set about settling her stepfather and her mother for the night.

She went to bed after that and, contrary to her expectations, slept at once. But she woke in the early hours, her mind very clear.

'It's funny I didn't think of it sooner. Of course I wanted to explain to him—because I'm in love with him.'

She felt a warm glow of happiness at the thought, but in the pale early-morning light common sense took over; the glow was still there but she must learn to keep it tucked away, out of sight and mind.

CHAPTER FOUR

FOR the next few days the hope that she would see Mr ter Breukel again coloured Sarah's dull daily round. She didn't sleep well, but each morning she got out of bed telling herself that surely he would phone her, or even come to say goodbye before he went back to Holland. And each night she went to bed and wept quietly. Not because she had hoped that they would meet again, but because he had seemed so pleased that she was, as he'd presumed, to marry Robert.

He would think nothing of her for keeping Robert up her sleeve, as it were, while accepting his friendship. And that was all it was, she reminded herself; she didn't expect anything warmer than that, but to have him as a friend would have been a wonderful thing.

Loving someone who didn't love you, reflected Sarah one night, mopping her eyes and blowing her small red nose, was very painful. She gave a great sniff and curled up in bed, wondering where he was and what he was doing. It was comforting, somehow, to know that somewhere out there, in the world she had so little chance of seeing much of, he would be working and eating and sleeping just as she was.

Which was exactly what he was doing. But, unlike her, he viewed the future in a different light. If Sarah was happy, if she wanted to marry this young doctor, then he would accept that, but first he had to be quite sure that this was so, and he *wasn't* sure...

Unlike Sarah, his days were full; he thrust her image to the back of his mind and dealt with consultations, clinics, patients and sessions in the operating theatre, as at home in the

London hospitals as he was at Arnhem. He had been a consultant at both hospitals for some years now, and came to London several times a year. Nevertheless he did have opportunities to drive to Clapham Common and see Sarah, all of which he ignored.

If she were going to marry Robert then she would have little interest in another visit from him, and the thin thread of their friendship might snap. And he must still find out more about her and Robert; only when he knew with certainty that they were to marry would he abandon his hopes for the future.

Two weeks later, on the point of his return to Arnhem, he telephoned Dr Benson, enquired as to Mr Holt's progress and, after a brief discussion, observed with just the right amount of interest that he had met the doctor's young partner.

Dr Benson was enthusiastic about him. 'A good doctor, and already well liked by my patients. He's getting married shortly—his future wife, Jennie, is a very nice girl, familiar with this area, too. They're busy getting their flat ready. They intended to marry next year, but since they've found this place and he's settled in so well there's no reason for them not to set up home sooner. Some time in May, I believe. If you're over here by any chance you must come to the wedding—and take a look at Mr Holt at the same time. I quite understand that your commitments prevented you from seeing him this time, but I can assure you that your good work will be continued here.'

'I feel sure of that. And Mrs Holt and her daughter?'

'Mrs Holt is quite herself again, a nervous and delicate lady, as you no doubt know, depending very much upon her daughter. And Sarah seems none the worse for the accident. She is rather a quiet girl, and seems even quieter now. She really needs to be independent and leave home, but of course she has no training, and Mrs Holt relies upon her for everything. She meets very few young people...'

All of which Mr ter Breukel thought about deeply as he

took himself back to Arnhem. The overwhelming relief at discovering that it wasn't Sarah who was to marry Robert was overshadowed by concern for her happiness. His first impulse was to carry her off and marry her out of hand, but she might have other wishes as to her future. Probably she regarded him as a rather staid man to whom she owed gratitude.

She had told him something of her life, but very little about her own hopes for the future. For all he knew she might want to travel, become a career girl, go on the stage. He must, he told himself, on no account be impatient, and if possible think of some means whereby she might become independent and see something of the world, even if it were only another part of London. Only then would he find a way of resuming their friendship and finally marrying her.

He needed to think about it, but only after he had tackled the backlog of patients and operations waiting for him at St Bravo's.

That done, he set about his problem with calm logic. Suzanne first, for he wanted her opinion of the prospects of a job for a girl without any kind of training.

She said at once, 'Oh, you're thinking of Sarah. Why don't you marry her, Litrik? Then she won't need to get work.'

'That's an easy answer, my dear. But Sarah's never had a chance to spread her wings. Suppose she were to marry me and then discover that what she wanted was a career of some sort, a chance to meet people—men—of her own age? No, she must have a little time to discover what she really wants.'

Suzanne thought. 'Well, I'd look for a job where all that was needed was common sense and a willingness to do anything wanted.' She shrugged. 'Sounds hopeless, doesn't it?'

'No, it makes sense. It will have to be work where I can keep her under my eye.'

'What about the hospital—the London one?'

'I had thought of that, and that is a possibility, but I have to find a way to get her there…'

Suzanne gave him a sisterly peck on the cheek. 'And you will, Litrik. Let me know if I can help, won't you?'

Mr ter Breukel had many friends, some of them colleagues of long standing at the London hospital. He was on good terms with the hospital manager, too, and it was through him, by asking carefully casual questions, that he discovered that there was a shortage of unskilled labour in the kitchens, the house doctors' rooms and dining room, and in the staff canteen.

The kitchens wouldn't do at all, and nor would the house doctors' quarters; he wasn't so old that he couldn't remember that young housemen tended to relax like small boys when they had the chance… It would have to be the canteen.

Having settled that, his next problem was somewhat harder to solve. How to get her away from Clapham Common? He ignored her stepfather—the man was a bully, and lacking in any kind feeling towards her, but he wouldn't be able to stop Sarah leaving home. It was her mother who would do that if she could, playing upon Sarah's kind heart and her sense of duty. Mr ter Breukel sat at his desk night after night, with the faithful Max at his feet, and bent his powerful brain to the matter.

To good effect. The series of telephone calls he eventually made were entirely satisfactory, even though they were protracted and necessitated a good deal of discussion. The impossible, reflected Mr ter Breukel, is sometimes possible, provided one is determined enough. And he *was* determined.

Mr Holt's leg confining him to the house and depriving Mrs Holt of participating in their normal social life meant that she was unable to enjoy herself as she would wish. She had friends—but friends who were loath to invite her to dinner parties without her husband, unwilling for her to join in their usual social round on her own. She had to fall back on bridge afternoons and shopping and the occasional meeting for coffee while shopping. As a consequence her discontent grew, as did her peevishness, and since there was no one else she vented both on Sarah.

'It is a pity that you're not pretty and socially minded,' she complained, 'then at least there would be some young people about the house.'

To which Sarah said nothing, although she could have pointed out that young people had never been encouraged. She remembered with shame the few occasions when she had invited schoolfriends home and watched her mother with subtle charm eclipse her own efforts. Later on it had been worse, for such young men as she'd met had occasionally found her mother's pretty ways and gentle manner quite irresistible...

Now, as far as she could see, the faint hopes that she could persuade her mother to let her find work were fading. Sarah had brought the matter up already, on several occasions, and her mother had told her with a pitiful smile that she must please herself; no mother would prevent her child from doing what they wished, however selfish that child was.

The days seemed endless to Sarah, although she didn't allow her despondency to get the upper hand. She had plenty to do—shopping, helping with the ironing and cooking, giving Mrs Twist a hand around the house, paying dutiful visits to her stepfather, listening to her mother's complaining voice. Days in which she had very little time to herself.

And a good thing too, she told herself; if she had time on her hands she would waste it thinking about Mr ter Breukel, who, she assured herself a dozen times a day, meant nothing to her. She would, in time, be able to discard her love for him. She reflected that it was probably a flash in the pan, engendered by her lack of men-friends. Probably she would have fallen in love with the first man she met, given the circumstances...

It was April now, quite warm and sunny. Sarah was in the garden, casting an eye over the tubs she had planted in the autumn, when Mrs Twist called her indoors.

'Yer ma wants yer, Miss Sarah. Very excited about something.'

Mrs Holt was in her bedroom, sitting at the dressing table, making up her pretty face. 'Sarah—get my new grey dress for me. I've had a phone call from Dr Benson. He's bringing some important specialist to see your stepfather. For heaven's sake, tidy yourself, and then go and get coffee ready. They'll be here in half an hour.'

'Didn't you say they're coming to see my stepfather?'

'Yes. But they'll want to know how *I* am. I'm sure I'll never be the same again after that horrible accident.' She glanced at Sarah. 'Get the coffee ready first, Sarah, then do something to your hair. *You* won't need to see them, of course, but I suppose you'll bring in the coffee.'

Sarah paused at the door. 'Mother, if you don't want me to be seen, you could fetch the coffee from the kitchen yourself.'

'Sarah, what a dreadful way to speak to your mother. You know how delicate my nerves are.' Mrs Holt touched a handkerchief to a dry eye. 'Now I'm upset.'

Sarah went away and got the tray ready, with the best china and a little dish of assorted biscuits. She popped two into her mouth and crossed the hall to the cloakroom. The breeze in the garden had ruffled her tidy hair, and she supposed that she had better run a comb through it. She was halfway across the hall when the doorbell was rung. She glanced at the long case clock by the stairs; it was far too soon for Dr Benson and this specialist—the postman, maybe, or someone trying to make a living selling dusters at the door? She opened the door and came face to face with Dr Benson.

'Oh, hello,' said Sarah. 'You're early. Mother said half an hour.' She smiled at him, for they were old friends, and then looked past him to the youngish man standing quietly behind him.

'This is Professor Smythe. I thought it a good idea if he were to cast an eye over your stepfather. And perhaps your mother would be glad of a word?'

Sarah held out a hand. 'I'm sure Mother and my stepfather will be glad to see you. Do come in.' She led the way to the drawing room. 'I'll fetch Mother. Would you like a cup of coffee?'

'Perhaps after we have seen Mr Holt?' Dr Benson looked at the professor, who nodded. 'Ah, here is your mother.'

Mrs Holt's voice could be heard through the half-open door, wanting to know who had rung the doorbell and why hadn't Sarah told her? She sounded cross, but as she came into the room and saw the two men she smiled charmingly. 'Dr Benson, how kind of you to come...' She turned to the professor and smiled even more charmingly. 'And this is the consultant you mentioned?'

'Professor Smythe, Mrs Holt. He will examine Mr Holt and give me any necessary advice.'

'I have been so anxious about him,' said Mrs Holt, offering a hand. 'I'm sure you're terribly clever. It was such a shock—the accident, you know. I feel that I shall never completely recover.'

The professor murmured. He would have a lovely bedside manner, thought Sarah, watching him from the door and then watching the three of them go upstairs to her stepfather's room. She didn't know if her mother had told Mr Holt of the impending visit, but whether he knew or not he would be annoyed by it.

They were upstairs for a long time. Sarah, keeping the coffee hot in the kitchen, ate two more biscuits, and when they finally came downstairs, she carried the tray into the drawing room. The professor took it from her with a smile, and sat down opposite Mrs Holt, while Sarah passed round cups and the biscuits.

'Sarah, run along, dear. I'm sure you don't want to be bored with our talk. Besides, I want a little chat with these two kind men. I've made light of my troubles, but I do feel that I need professional help.'

Sarah didn't say anything, but the professor put his cup and saucer down and went to open the door for her. She looked at him as she went past. He had a kind face and was smiling.

She shared a pot of tea with Mrs Twist and, since she had nothing else to do, sat at the kitchen table chopping up vegetables for the casserole which Mrs Twist was intending to cook.

They were a long time, she thought uneasily, then looked up as the door opened and Professor Smythe came in.

Sarah jumped up. 'Have you lost your way? The drawing room's on the other side of the house—down the passage and across the hall.'

'No. No, I wish to talk to you.' He glanced at Mrs Twist and smiled, and that lady put down the knife with which she had been cutting up the meat.

'You'd best stay here,' she said. 'I've plenty to get on with upstairs.'

He opened the door for her and thanked her with another smile, and then pulled out a chair and sat down opposite Sarah.

'You really shouldn't be here in the kitchen,' said Sarah. 'I mean, you're a professor...'

'I like kitchens.' He had a pleasant voice, very quiet. 'We always have breakfast in our kitchen; it's so much easier with two small children.'

'Boys or girls?'

'One of each, soon to be joined by a third.'

'How nice... I mustn't waste your time. Did you want to tell me something? Is Mother ill?' she asked worriedly.

'Your mother is in the best of health, but I have suggested certain changes which might improve her physically and mentally.'

When Sarah gave him a questioning look he said, 'Your mother is bored; she needs a complete change in her lifestyle. Dr Benson and I have had a chat and he fully endorses my suggestion that your mother and stepfather should close the house for a period and spend time at a hotel, somewhere where your mother can enjoy something of a social life. Your stepfather can be given all the attention he wants—massage, daily visits from a nurse—for a gradual return to the full use of his leg. I suggested Bournemouth—good hotels, shops, entertainment, access to private nursing facilities. I understand that there will be no financial problems...'

Sarah opened her mouth, closed it, and shook her head. She didn't speak but her eyes looked a question.

'Your mother agrees with me that a fresh environment and new faces would be ideal, and I suggested that she would benefit greatly from meeting people about whom she knew nothing and who knew nothing of her and your stepfather. I think that it would be wise if you do not go with them, and your mother has been persuaded that this is the right thing to do.'

'I don't have to go, too? I can stay here with Mrs Twist?' Sarah beamed at him. 'For how long? You're sure Mother won't change her mind and I'd have to go, too?'

'Quite sure, and we've suggested a period of two to three months.'

He watched her face light up. A plain girl, but nice eyes, and when she smiled she looked almost beautiful. No wonder Litrik was interested in her. The things one does for one's old friends, reflected Professor Smythe.

'Dr Benson has made a most sensible suggestion,' he went on smoothly. 'Why not get a job while you are here with the housekeeper? It will fill your days, and you will meet people and earn some money.'

'I'd like that very much, but you see I'm not trained for anything. When I left school Mother wasn't very well, and she gets very upset if I suggest leaving home.'

'Then why not take this opportunity to try your hand at something? There are jobs which require little or no training, you know. I'm sure Dr Benson can advise you.'

Sarah sat up straight in her chair. 'Oh, my goodness, wouldn't it be absolutely marvellous?' She sounded like a schoolgirl, he thought, and looked like one too in her skirt and sweater. He had noticed that Mrs Holt was dressed fashionably. Either her daughter had no dress sense, or no money with which to buy pretty clothes. He had formed a low opinion of her stepfather—not a man to open a generous purse.

'Then shall we go and tell your mother that you agree with us that a short period in new surroundings will be beneficial to her health?'

Sarah said yes; he sounded exactly as a professor should sound, very sure of himself.

Her mother was talking animatedly to Dr Benson, but broke off to exclaim, 'Sarah, is this not a splendid idea of these two kind gentlemen? And your stepfather has agreed. You won't blame your poor little mother for leaving you alone for a few weeks? You will have Mrs Twist. I know that we shall return completely cured and able to resume our normal lives again.'

Sarah eyed her mother with patient tolerance. 'It's a splendid idea, Mother. I shall be quite all right here with Mrs Twist.'

'That's what I thought, dear. There must be many things you want to do, and now you will have the time.'

Sarah agreed pleasantly, and tried not to look too pleased.

The two men left presently, and her mother went to discuss their plans with her husband. So Sarah went to the kitchen and gave Mrs Twist an account of the doctor's visit, leaving

out the news that she intended to go to work. Mrs Twist was
a dear soul, and her staunch friend, but there was just a chance
that she might inadvertently let the cat out of the bag.

Now that the decision had been taken, Mrs Holt lost no
time. Hotel brochures were scanned, dates were decided upon,
and a good deal of shopping was done—for a new environment needed new clothes. It was left to Sarah to search out
a nursing agency who would send a nurse and a masseuse
each day to the hotel, and it was she who booked rooms at
a splendid hotel on the seafront. When it came to his own
comfort, her stepfather spent lavishly, and just as lavishly but
rather less willingly on his wife.

He was less concerned for Sarah. He arranged for expenses
for the household to be paid weekly, together with Mrs
Twist's wages, and in a sudden display of generosity told
Sarah that if she needed money for any other reason she could
ask him for it.

'As long as it's a reasonable amount,' he cautioned her.
'This is an expensive undertaking. If anyone at the office
should need me urgently, refer them to me.'

Mr ter Breukel, kept up to date by his friend Professor
Smythe, was satisfied. The next step would be taken by Dr
Benson, primed by him after another satisfactory phone call
to the hospital manager in London.

Mr ter Breukel possessed his soul in patience and waited
for the next move in his scheme.

The removal to Bournemouth was almost as big an undertaking as the journey back from Holland had been. Mr Holt had
a new car now, and a hired chauffeur, and between them he
and Mrs Holt had a vast quantity of luggage. And the business
of getting him comfortable with a leg still in a small plaster
took time and the efforts of several persons. But at last he
pronounced himself satisfied, Sarah's mother got in beside

him, the chauffeur got behind the wheel and drove away. Sarah and Mrs Twist waved, but went unnoticed.

The pair of them went back to the kitchen, and over a pot of tea Sarah told her plans. 'Of course I have to find a job,' she explained, 'and that might take a few days. You won't mind? I'll find work where I can come home each evening. Oh, Mrs Twist, it's the chance I've always hoped for and never thought I'd get—not without running away in the middle of the night. But that wouldn't have been very practical…'

Mrs Twist pronounced the scheme a good one. 'High time a young lady like you got out and about a bit—never a moment to yourself. What'll yer do?'

'I've no idea…' But she was soon to find out.

It was two days later when Dr Benson called. Sarah was in the kitchen, working her way through the 'Jobs Vacant' columns of several newspapers. She had already searched the adverts in *The Lady* magazine, and marked several likely posts, but most of them were out of London. The local paper might be more fruitful. She looked up as Mrs Twist ushered the doctor into the kitchen and got to her feet.

'Dr Benson—is something wrong? Mother? My stepfather?'

'No, no, Sarah, my visit concerns yourself. You do remember we talked about you finding a job?' His eye fell on the pile of newspapers. 'You're looking for something? Well, unless you've arranged anything, I've heard of something you might care to try. Perhaps not quite your touch, but it would give you a start if you really want to strike out on your own.'

'Oh, I do. I'll do anything—well, not computers or typing or anything clever, and I don't think I'd be much good in a shop…'

'No skill needed for this job. Just patience and a friendly manner and an ability to stay on your feet for hours.' At her questioning look he added, 'The canteen at one of the hospitals is desperately short of staff. Serving meals, clearing away, fetching and carrying. Long hours, and shift work—twelve o'clock until eight in the evening, five days a week—but you wouldn't have to work on Saturday or Sunday. It's not much, I know, but you would meet people, Sarah, and it seems to me that that is something you have never had the chance of doing, other than your mother's bridge partners and your stepfather's business acquaintances.' He added, 'The pay's not much...'

When he told her she said, 'Not much? And I can spend it on myself, clothes and things?'

'Of course. Look, I'll give you the phone number and you can ask for an interview. Here's the number. Use my name as a reference and don't go looking too smart.'

Sarah said matter-of-factly, 'I haven't any smart clothes. And thank you very much; I shall phone this morning.' She laughed suddenly. 'It's the first step towards my marvellous future.'

Dr Benson agreed. He hoped that Mr ter Breukel's schemes wouldn't go awry. He was pushing his luck, giving her the opportunity to savour an independent life. Would it not have been better to have snapped her up at once and carried her off to Holland? On second thoughts, Dr Benson felt not. Sarah, for all her unassuming ways, had always refused to be led, and her stepfather's dislike of her hadn't helped.

Sarah believed in striking while the iron was hot; she phoned the moment Dr Benson had left the house, and was given an appointment for the next morning.

It wasn't until she had entered the rather gloomy portals of the hospital that doubts assailed her. She was to be interviewed by someone called the Domestic Supervisor. She might be disliked on sight; her references might not be sufficient to please this personage. By the time Sarah had reached the door to which she had been directed, the Domestic Supervisor had become the female equivalent of an ogre!

The voice which bade her enter was small and high-

pitched, and to her relief Sarah saw that her imagined ogre
was a very small, very round woman, with salt and pepper
hair screwed into a bun and a nice smile.

'Come in, dearie. Miss Beckwith, isn't it? Sit down while
we have a little chat.'

Fifteen minutes later Sarah rose from the chair. The job
was hers. She was to start on the following day at noon.

'You may find it a bit of a rush for a day or two, but the
girls will help you. You'll get your dinner at two o'clock, tea
at five. The canteen closes down then, until first suppers at
seven o'clock, but you'll be kept busy getting them ready.
Second supper is at eight o'clock, and that's when the night
shift take over. Hard work, my dear, but we'll see how you
get on, shall we? A week's notice on either side.'

Sarah went back to Clapham Common and told Mrs Twist
all about it. They arranged their days to suit them both. 'And
if by any chance my mother should ring up, would you just
tell her I'm out? But I don't expect her to telephone during
the day.'

'Wear comfortable shoes,' advised Mrs Twist. 'Your feet
are going to kill you.'

They didn't kill her, but by the end of her shift they ached
so much she thought that she would never be able to go to
work the next morning. But that was in a weak moment; lying
in a hot bath, after supper with Mrs Twist, she knew that of
course she would go to work in the morning. What was more,
she would continue to do so until she found better work.

She had enjoyed her day, she reflected, adding more hot
water. Dressed in a striped cotton dress, a white pinny and a
white cap, she had presented herself to the Head Counter
Assistant, admitted cheerfully that she had very little idea as
to what she had to do, and had been borne away by two
middle-aged women who'd called her 'ducks', showed her
where everything was and, when the food arrived, stood her
in front of a great container of chips. 'Dole 'em out, and no

need to be mean about it. A couple of spoons and a bit over.
Give us a shout if yer in a fix.'

She had managed very well; it seemed that everyone ate
chips, and some of the housemen on duty, unable to get to
their own dining room, had had two helpings. And everyone
had been so friendly, asking her name, making little jokes.
Though it had shaken her a bit when she had been dishing
out chips to a bunch of nurses, standing there with their plates
and discussing an accident case which had been admitted that
morning. Sarah had tried not to hear the details. Nurses, she'd
thought, must be wonderful people—able to take the sight of
broken bones and blood everywhere, and still pile their plates
with a wholesome dinner....

The only part of her day which she hadn't enjoyed was
coming home. It was quite a long journey to and from the
hospital, and although the April evenings were light, by the
time she'd got off the bus evening had closed in, and the five-
minute walk to her home was through more or less deserted
streets. But that was something to which she would become
accustomed; she had never had the chance to be out on her
own in the evenings, only in her mother's company, or going
with her and her stepfather to some function when he considered it good for his public image to be seen as a kindly stepfather and devoted husband.

By the end of the week her feet had accustomed themselves
to standing for long periods, she had learnt her way around
the canteen, made friends with the other girls and was on
nodding terms with the hungry hordes who came to eat. They
were always in a hurry, either on duty, or off duty and hurrying to get away. She exchanged rather guarded chat with
anyone who lingered to talk for a moment, and took care to
note which of the ward sisters liked a salad instead of vegetables.

She was always famished by two o'clock, but none of them
wasted much time over their meal; there was tea to get ready,

the first of the staff would start trickling in at about half past three, and after a brief pause there would be a second round of tea...and then a rush to get suppers on the counter.

But she had enjoyed it. She had met more people in a week than she had in all the years since she left school, and she had a pay packet in her pocket. What mattered most was that she had been so busy that she had been able to banish Mr ter Breukel from her thoughts for minutes at a time...

She took Mrs Twist out to supper on Saturday evening, to a small restaurant in the High Street, and Mrs Twist, in a hat suitable to the occasion, ate her way through the three-course meal and pronounced it as well cooked as she herself could have done. 'A real treat,' she declared, 'eating something I haven't 'ad to cook meself.'

On Sunday Mrs Twist went to spend the day with her sister; Sarah washed her hair and her smalls, did her nails, read the Sunday papers from end to end and thought about Mr ter Breukel. Mrs Twist safely back, they had their supper and went to bed.

'I shall never see him again,' said Sarah, looking at the moon through a sudden rush of tears. She wiped them away at once, told herself not to be a sentimental fool and got into bed.

It was halfway through her second week, as she was on the point of going down to the basement to start another day's work, that the lift door beside the staircase opened and Mr ter Breukel got out.

He had seen her, of course. 'Ah, Sarah, how nice to see you again.'

Her heart was beating so loudly he must surely be able to hear it. She had gone very red, and then pale, and hadn't said a word.

She found her breath. 'I shall be late,' she told him, and flew down the stairs.

He stood watching her race away, smiling to himself. She

reminded him of the White Rabbit in *Alice in Wonderland*. He glanced at his watch; she would be off duty at eight o'clock. He had a clinic that afternoon, and post-operative patients to see later, but he would be free by then.

Everyone in the canteen acknowledged that Sarah was a good worker, willing to help out and not afraid of hard work, but today she surpassed herself: she served the meals, cleaned the tables and laid them again, swabbed the floor where some-one had upset a bottle of tomato sauce, even offered to stay on for an extra hour or two as they were short-handed that day. An offer which wasn't accepted.

'You've worked yourself to death,' it was pointed out to her. 'You'll go off at eight sharp and no nonsense.'

All the same she was held up at the last minute by one of the staff coming in for sandwiches for the operating theatre staff, so that when she got to the changing room everyone else had gone.

She'd had some half-formed idea that if she went out of the hospital in a bunch with the other girls and saw Mr ter Breukel there would be no need to speak to him. Indeed, she could pretend not to see him... Now she would have to hope that he would be gone or, better still, in Theatre, operating.

She changed rapidly and climbed the stairs to the ground floor, taking the last few steps with all the wariness of a rabbit coming out of its burrow. The corridor was empty; she skimmed down it and saw that there was no one in the en-trance hall. It was a relief not to meet him, although she ached with disappointment. Just that one glimpse of him coming out of the lift had been enough to undo all her sternly suppressed feelings since she had last seen him.

She called goodnight to the porter and pushed open the heavy doors. April had turned contrary; it was cold and windy and heavy clouds threatened rain. She paused to button her coat collar, and found herself face to face with Mr ter Breukel.

For the second time that day she lost her tongue, staring

up at his face, trying to think of something suitable to say. Hello was a bit too familiar; good evening sounded all wrong. 'It's not a very nice evening,' said Sarah.

'Very unpleasant,' he agreed cheerfully. 'Shall we have a meal out, or go to your place?'

'But they're not there—Mother and my stepfather. They're in Bournemouth recuperating.'

'Indeed? Then let us find a restaurant.'

'No, no, I can't. I mean, it's very kind of you to ask me, but Mrs Twist's waiting for me with supper. She'll wonder where I am.'

'Then let us go to Clapham Common and perhaps you will invite me to supper?'

Sarah, mindful of her manners, invited him, then added, 'Why are you here?'

He popped her into the car and got in beside her. 'I come here to work fairly frequently. You're working at the hospital?'

'Yes. Dr Benson and a Professor Smythe came to see my stepfather, and they thought it would do him and mother good to go away for a while. So they're in Bournemouth, and since I'm at home with Mrs Twist Dr Benson suggested that I got a job.' She added defiantly, 'I serve the meals at the canteen.'

'You enjoy that? Meeting new faces, making friends? You must have missed that, Sarah?'

'Yes. When Mother and my stepfather come back I shall move out—find a room, get a better job if I can, train for something.'

She glanced at his hands on the wheel and looked away quickly. They were large, beautifully kept, and they reminded her how very much she loved him.

He parked the car outside the house and went in with her. Mrs Twist, coming into the hall, gave him a shrewd look as Sarah introduced them.

'Pleased ter meet yer, I'm sure,' she told him, and took the hand that he held out. 'Staying for supper? It's steak and kidney pie and apple turnovers. Miss Sarah, you go into the drawing room and have a drink while I lay the table.'

Sarah frowned. 'Mrs Twist—it's all ready in the kitchen, isn't it?'

'I like kitchens,' said Mr ter Breukel, and smiled at Mrs Twist.

'Well, then, if you say so, sir.'

'I'll get the sherry,' said Sarah, and went to the drawing room.

Mr ter Breukel followed her, took the bottle from her, dropped a kiss on her cheek and said quietly, 'We must find time to talk, but not just yet.'

He smiled down at her. 'The pie smells delicious. Come and tell me about your job while we eat.'

CHAPTER FIVE

MRS TWIST was at first reluctant to eat her supper with Sarah and Mr ter Breukel. 'I know me place,' she had said sharply, but then under his kindly eye she had changed her mind.

'Well, if that's what you want, sir. I should've thought you'd want ter be on yer own, like, with Miss Sarah.'

'Ah, but you see Sarah and I have all the time in the world to be together.'

A remark which caused Sarah to give him a surprised look, which he met with a bland smile. He was putting Mrs Twist at her ease, she reflected.

The meal was a success; Mrs Twist was a great talker, and Mr ter Breukel was adept at maintaining a conversation, and if Sarah was rather silent no one noticed. They didn't hurry over it, and when it was eaten Mr ter Breukel accepted Mrs Twist's offer of a cup of tea with every appearance of pleasure, drinking the powerful brew with evident appreciation before helping to clear the table and then making his departure, saying all the right things to Mrs Twist, bidding Sarah a friendly goodnight, and driving away without fuss.

While Mrs Twist washed up Sarah set the table for breakfast.

'Now there's a man for you,' said Mrs Twist. 'A real gent, even if 'e is a bit of a la-di-da. Fancy me eating me supper with the likes of 'im. Whatever would your ma say?'

'Well, she won't know,' said Sarah. 'I shan't tell, and you won't either.'

'Lor' bless you, no. Known 'im long?'

'Well, I don't really know him very well. He looked after

my stepfather at the Arnhem hospital; he's a Consultant there too, as well as over here.'

'A bit lonely over here on his own?' Mrs Twist was dying of curiosity.

'I don't suppose so. He's well known at the hospital, I think, and he must have lots of friends.'

'Well, I dare say you'll see a bit more of 'im while 'e's 'ere.'

'I doubt it,' said Sarah. 'The senior staff don't come to the canteen.'

But they were in the same building, she reflected, and if she took the long way round to the canteen she might see him.

During the next few days, though, there wasn't so much as a glimpse of him. You wouldn't think, thought Sarah, that such a large man could become so invisible. And he *was* in the hospital; dishing dinners to a group of staff nurses, she couldn't help but overhear their gossip. Mr ter Breukel, it seemed, had won the hearts of all the nurses who had had the good fortune to encounter him.

Sarah swallowed a sharp pang of jealousy and told herself not to be a fool. The sooner he went back to Holland the better, she decided. Life would never be the same again without him, but at least she could make a new life for herself now that she had work. She wasn't sure what would be the next step, but she was determined that it would be up, taking her away from Clapham Common. A month or two more working in the canteen, and then she would apply for the night shift; the pay was better. Several of the girls had rooms close to the hospital; she would do the same, save what money she could, and look for a better job.

She told herself that she was happy and content, that the future was exciting; she would become a successful career woman. She had no idea how this was to be achieved, but the thought of it made her days bearable as each successive one went by without a sight of Mr ter Breukel.

And when at last she saw him again it was disastrous. It was the end of her shift, and, last as usual, she climbed the stairs with one of the housemen who had been to the canteen to gobble a hasty supper. He was a nice lad, and lonely, and so was she. They dawdled up the staircase, making the most of a few moments of idle conversation, not really interested in each other, only glad to talk to someone.

They lingered on the top step, reluctant to go their separate ways, and Mr ter Breukel, intent on whisking Sarah out for a meal, came to an abrupt silent halt. Sarah was laughing and the young doctor laughed too, enjoying the small interlude, and instead of going straight to the wards he turned to walk to the entrance with her, still talking.

It was then that Sarah saw Mr ter Breukel, walking towards them, and she paused in mid-sentence, smiling her delight at the sight of him.

A pity he didn't know that; he went past them with a brief, unsmiling nod and turned into the consultants' room, shutting the door firmly behind him.

Sarah parted with her companion in the entrance hall, hardly aware of how she had got there. Mr ter Breukel could have smiled, even wished her good evening. Perhaps he didn't care to be on speaking terms with a member of the domestic staff. She dismissed that thought as unworthy of him, left the hospital and walked to the bus stop.

There was no reason, she told herself, why he *should* speak to her. He was doubtless a busy man; moreover, he must have many friends in London. Taking her home the other evening had been an impulsive gesture which he clearly didn't intend to repeat.

Mr ter Breukel closed the door gently, quelling a desire to slam it or wrench it open again and pluck Sarah away from the cheerful young man with her. He would like to shake her until her teeth rattled. Better still, he would like to wrap his arms round her and kiss her.

He did none of these things, but went and sat down in one of the leather chairs arranged round the sombre room. He had no reason to be angry; he had planned this deliberately so that Sarah would have a chance to be independent and meet people. Well, his plan was working. It was early days, though, he reminded himself. He must have patience still, leave her free to choose her friends, plan her future. He was deeply in love with her, but he wanted her to be happy even at the cost of his own happiness.

So the best part of another week went by; he would be returning to Holland soon now...

As for Sarah, she felt herself to be a seasoned worker now, with little time to brood. Only at the weekends, alone in the house while Mrs Twist visited friends or family, did she admit to herself that life wasn't very satisfactory. It would be better, of course, once she could forget Mr ter Breukel...

One Friday evening, her pay packet in her pocket, she left the hospital rather later than usual. There had been no one in the cloakroom to tell her that there was a rowdy demonstration over something or other making its way towards the streets around the hospital, and the porter, deep in his evening paper, hadn't seen her slip out of the doors. The other canteen staff had left in a bunch, so he had warned them, thinking that they were all there. It was only as the doors swung back that he looked up and caught a glimpse of Sarah, hurrying away. Too late to go after her, he decided, and someone would have told her to avoid the main roads.

Mr ter Breukel, on the point of departure, having done a ward round and taken a look at his operation cases for that day, spoke to the ward sister, wishing her good evening and a pleasant weekend. She remarked, 'I expect you've heard that there's some kind of demonstration coming this way, sir? Most of it is peaceful enough, but there are the usual rowdies roaming around, making trouble. The staff going off duty have been warned to avoid them.'

Mr ter Breukel glanced at the clock. Ten minutes past eight. Sarah would have left or be on the point of leaving. He bade Sister a courteous goodnight and went down to the entrance hall.

The porter put his paper down and stood up. Mr ter Breukel had that effect upon people, although he was unconscious of it.

'The canteen staff?' he asked. 'Have they left?'

'Yes, a minute or two after eight o'clock. I passed on the warning that they should keep clear of any disturbances.'

'And no one has left since?'

'Well, now you mention it, sir, someone slipped out while I had my back turned. She was halfway across the forecourt before I heard the door close.'

'You have no idea who it was?'

'No, sorry, sir, only she wasn't very big and she had a red umbrella.' He added unnecessarily, 'It's raining, sir.'

Mr ter Breukel thanked him politely and went out into the drizzle, walking fast. He knew which bus stop Sarah used, and he had seen the red umbrella before. He searched the queue there. There was no sign of her; she was already on her way home, then. He turned away and saw a red umbrella a long way ahead of him, and at the same time several groups of noisy youths marching arm-in-arm on the pavement, pushing aside all the people.

He lengthened his stride, ignoring the catcalls, pushing and shoving. The pavement was almost empty of other people, who were prudently taking cover in doorways and shops. Sarah was in plain sight, and why she was ignoring the fracas around her was something he couldn't understand—until he saw that she was with someone, another woman, and that they were both burdened with shopping bags.

There were some side roads lined by small brick houses, their doors opening onto the pavement. He saw Sarah turn into one such road and reached the corner of it only a few yards behind her. The road was empty save for three youths running from its other end, swooping down on her and her companion, yelling and shouting. The woman dropped her shopping bags and struggled to open the door of a house, but she dropped the key from a shaking hand as the three youths rushed at them.

Sarah furled her umbrella and poked the nearest boy in the ribs, then she thumped his companion and would have done the same for the third, but he caught it and tore it from her hand, waved it wildly and swung it down...

It didn't reach its mark; Mr ter Breukel swept Sarah aside with one arm, lifted the youth by his coat collar and set him down in a sprawling heap on the pavement, then sent the other two tumbling after him.

They stared up at him; he might look like a gentleman, but he was certainly a giant, and for all they knew a prizefighter in his best suit out for a stroll. They edged themselves backwards, scrambled to their feet and rushed away.

Mr ter Breukel hadn't said a word; he wasn't breathing fast either. He stooped, picked up the key and handed it to the woman, and then, since she was still all of a tremble, took it from her, opened the door and stood aside for her to go in. He handed in her shopping bags too, assuring her that she was now quite safe, then brushed aside her thanks, waiting patiently while she thanked Sarah at some length and at last closed her door.

Only then did he turn to Sarah, standing rather quiet and pale beside him.

'Much as I commend your bravery, Sarah, I must beg you

never to risk your safety again—I cannot keep an eye on you all the time...'

'Keep an eye on me?' Her voice was rather shrill, what with indignation and delayed fright. 'I haven't seen you for days.'

Mr ter Breukel sighed. 'No, and for several good reasons. The answer is for us to get married.'

'Well, you may if you wish,' snapped Sarah. 'I'll have to wait until someone asks me.'

'If you would just listen, you silly girl. I *am* asking you.'

She looked at him as though he had lost his wits; the drizzle had ceased, there was even a patch or two of blue sky, but the wind was cold and she shivered, as much with the chilliness as the shock of his words.

'You're asking me?'

He was leaning against the door; now he drew her to stand beside him and put an arm around her shoulders.

'Yes, I am, but let me explain.' He paused, before going on carefully, 'It had occurred to me that we would be happy together as man and wife, but I felt—still do feel—that you should first have the opportunity of finding your feet away from home. You have had no chance to do so, have you? You would have continued to live at home, tied to your mother's every wish and whim, disliked by and disliking your stepfather, gradually losing heart and becoming resigned. You see, Sarah, other girls might run away, but you have too tender a heart. But now you have discovered independence, and perhaps you want to spread your wings?'

She found her voice. 'You want to marry me? But you don't know anything about me, do you? And—and you don't love me...'

'Have I not said that I believe we could be happy together? And if you wished to have a career of some sort I wouldn't stand in your way; you would be free to follow your own interests.'

She stared into his calm face. He sounded so kind and so reasonable, as though getting married was a simple act, shorn of all doubts. And his argument made sense too. But it wouldn't be simple at all, she reflected. She loved him, but he hadn't said that he loved her, and if she married him she had no wish to be anything other than his wife, behaving like other wives: being at home when he got home, seeing that he had nourishing meals and spotless linen, listening with a sympathetic ear to him after a hard day's work. And children— she wanted children—and she wanted him to love her...

She said slowly, 'I've never been asked to marry anyone before, so I'm not sure what to say.'

He smiled then. 'Then don't say anything. We will go back to the hospital and I'll drive you home. I shan't stay. Think about it as much as you wish, and when you're ready we'll talk again.'

He stopped himself just in time from kissing her, which was a pity, for it would have put an end to their misunderstanding. Instead he took her arm and walked her back through the almost quiet streets. There were a few people standing about, shopkeepers sweeping up broken glass, car owners examining damaged cars, the odd scuffle as police collected up the remnants of the street gangs.

Sarah was far too busy with her thoughts to notice any of these things. She got into the car and sat without speaking until they reached her home.

Mr ter Breukel got out, opened her door and stood beside her on the pavement.

'You said that you haven't seen me, Sarah. But do remember that I am always there.' He rang the doorbell, waited until Mrs Twist opened the door, and then went back to his car.

Sarah watched him drive away. She longed to marry him, but she wouldn't. He had said that they would be happy together, but supposing that he met a woman he loved? What then?

She followed Mrs Twist into the kitchen, and over supper gave her a watered-down version of the evening.

'A blessing that dear man went after you,' said Mrs Twist. 'A pity 'e couldn't stay for 'is supper.'

Sarah remembered then that she hadn't even offered him a cup of coffee. He had said that he couldn't stay, but she could at least have offered something.

She went to bed presently, and lay awake a long time, imagining life as his wife, until she went to sleep, only to wake in the morning knowing that she was going to refuse him.

She must think up some really good reason—a career in something or other—computers. She had been told that once one had mastered them, there were unending opportunities—super jobs, marvellous salaries, meeting important people. She would find out as much as possible about them so that she would sound convincing. And he would be secretly relieved, she felt sure.

She rehearsed several suitable speeches on her way to work on Monday; she must be ready to give him his answer when next they met—perhaps not that day, but certainly before the week was out. Satisfied that she couldn't improve upon them, she worked even harder than usual in her canteen, outwardly cheerful but with a heart grieving for what might have been.

She didn't see Mr ter Breukel that day, nor the next, and when she did see him again her carefully worded speeches went unspoken.

The letter which had come by that morning's post from her mother had for the moment driven all other thoughts out of her head. She had sat down to read it after breakfast, while Mrs Twist went to the shops. She had read it, and then read it again, not quite believing it.

The letter wasn't long, and a good deal of it was taken up with instructions. Mrs Holt wrote to say that they had decided to move to Bournemouth; they liked the town, they had made many friends, and they had seen a delightful house close to the sea. Her stepfather, went on Mrs Holt, intended to more or less retire, so he would need to go to London only very infrequently. The house at Clapham Common was to be sold, and Sarah and Mrs Twist were to remain in it until a buyer had been found, after which they could travel to Bournemouth. There would be no need for Mrs Holt to return for the moment. Sarah could deal with the estate agents and any prospective buyers, and she and Mrs Twist could start to pack away any silver and china not in use, together with her and Mr Holt's clothes.

Sarah, reading the letter yet again, had looked in vain for some comment as to how she and Mrs Twist might feel about it; her mother had taken it for granted that they would be happy to fall in with her plans. And Sarah was to tell Mrs Twist...

She'd decided to wait and tell the housekeeper when she got home that evening; they could discuss it at their leisure. Perhaps Mrs Twist would choose to go to Bournemouth, after all. But her relations and friends were scattered in and around London, so she might not want to. As for her self, Sarah knew that she would never go to Bournemouth.

But perhaps here was the solution to her problem; she could tell Mr ter Breukel that her mother and stepfather were moving from the Clapham Common house and wished her to join them. She would be able to find a job there, she would tell him, and meet any number of people. She wouldn't be telling a lie, she assured herself, just altering the truth a little, and as soon as he had gone back to Holland she would find other work.

It shouldn't be too hard; she would get a reference from the hospital, and she had been saving her wages. Not to marry him would break her heart, but even worse was the thought of marrying a man who didn't love her. Oh, he liked her, they were friends, and he had been unfailingly kind each time they had met, but that was no foundation for a marriage.

She rehearsed a number of now suitable speeches, and then, when they did meet, forgot them all.

They came face to face in the entrance hall, she on her way home, he on the way to check on his patients from his morning list in Theatre. It was no place in which to have a lengthy talk but he stopped in front of her, blocking her path with his bulk.

'Are you going home?' he asked without preamble. 'Because if you are may I come and see you later?'

Sarah said quickly, 'Can you spare five minutes now? I'll be very quick. I've had a letter from my mother. They're selling the house at Clapham Common and have bought one in Bournemouth. They want me to go and live with them there. It's a bit of a surprise, but it's like an answer, isn't it? I mean, I'll be able to start afresh, get a job, meet people.'

Mr ter Breukel's face showed none of his feelings; he said in a level voice, 'That is what you want, Sarah? You believe that this is really your chance to change your life, become independent? You would be happy?'

'Oh, yes,' said Sarah, and prayed for forgiveness for such a whopping lie. 'So you see there's no need for you to marry me.' She swallowed the lump in her throat. 'Thank you very much for asking me.'

He smiled. It was a bitter smile, but his voice was friendly enough. 'I must be glad that your future has become so promising. I'm sure you will make a success of whatever you choose to do.'

Sarah said, 'Yes, so there's no need for you to come this evening.' She looked up into his expressionless face. 'I wouldn't have liked you to have come all the way to Clapham just to hear that I'd decided to change my mind.'

He agreed gravely. So she *had* intended to marry him, had

she? And now she had changed her mind. He wondered why. Something he would find out.

They parted in a friendly fashion, going their separate ways, he to his patients, thrusting all thoughts of her from his mind for the moment, she to stand in a long queue for a bus, longing to get home so that she could go somewhere quiet and cry until she had no tears left.

She saw him two days later, passing him on her way to the basement stairs. He stopped, wished her a friendly good afternoon, and told her that he would be returning to Holland on the following day.

Sarah put out a hand and managed a smile. 'I hope you have a good journey. Will you be in Holland for a long time?'

'Three weeks—a month. Then back here very briefly. You will probably be gone by then.'

'Yes, I suppose so. Please give my love to Suzanne. And thank you for all your kindness.'

There was really nothing more to say. 'I'll be late,' she said, and raced down the stairs. Well, that's over, she told herself, I must get away from here before he comes back. Brave words, drowned in unshed tears.

Mrs Twist, informed of her employers' plans, had refused to go to Bournemouth; her family and friends were scattered around London and that was where she belonged. She'd agreed to stay at home until it was sold.

Mrs Holt had written Sarah another long letter demanding that she went to Bournemouth as quickly as possible so that she might accompany her mother on the shopping expeditions necessary for the new house. She was to pack up the ornaments and silver, and their clothes, and oversee the removal of a good deal of the furniture.

'Two weeks should be ample time for you to see to this,' the letter had said. 'We shall expect you no later than that.'

Mr ter Breukel had gone; Sarah gave in her notice and wrote and told her mother that she would see to the packing up of the things she wished for, and arrange for the furniture to be collected, but that she herself would be staying in London. 'I have a good job and somewhere to live,' she wrote recklessly, 'and I intend to become independent. I am sure that you and my stepfather will be very happy in your new home, but please understand that I would like to lead a life of my own...'

Naturally enough, this letter caused a flood of telephone calls and indignant letters, to which Sarah replied firmly. 'It isn't that I don't love you, Mother, as you suggest, but I do wish for my own life, and you must agree with me that my stepfather will be glad not to have me in the house. Once you are settled in, with a good housekeeper and everything to your liking, I'm sure that you will see the good sense of this. Later on, when I get my holidays, I will come and visit you.'

Mrs Twist, shocked at first at Sarah's decision, agreed that it was a chance which might never occur again. 'Just as long as yer get a good job...'

'Oh, I shall,' said Sarah airily. 'I'll stay here until I do. It may take a week or two until I find something I would like to do.'

Mrs Twist studied her face. 'Let's hope so. You look peaked, Miss Sarah, and you've got thin. That job at the hospital was too hard work.'

It had certainly been that, agreed Sarah silently, but Litrik had been there too. She thought about him constantly, and now she would never see him again she called him Litrik. It didn't matter any more; he had really gone out of her life, and now she had left the canteen there were no more snatches of gossip to be gleaned about him.

She began looking for work, setting about it in a dogged fashion, answering anything which sounded suitable for her meagre talents. But she had no luck; her letters were ignored, or she was told the job had been filled, and the few interviews she went to were unsuccessful. She had so few skills, and serving in a canteen, however good her reference was, wasn't enough.

Finally she found work, filling shelves at a supermarket. It was part-time, from half past seven in the morning until noon, and it was work she could do without needing anything other than an ability to work hard and quickly and to be honest. It was only a short bus ride from her home too, and although the wages weren't much she was able to save almost all of her pay packet since she was still living at home.

But there was a prospective buyer for the house, and she would need to earn more money if she had to find a bedsitter. She became a little thinner, and a little paler, and muddled in with her worries was the constant image of Litrik.

Sarah had been working at the supermarket for a week when Mr ter Breukel returned to London. And, being a man very much in love despite the hopelessness of the situation, he went straight to the hospital; he wanted to be sure that she was still intent on going to Bournemouth. He had no intention of giving up until she actually left London; indeed he had no intention of giving up even then.

He found his way to the Domestic Supervisor's office, exchanged civilities, and enquired if Sarah Beckwith was still working on the same shift.

The supervisor managed not to look surprised. Whatever next? A senior consultant seeking the whereabouts of one of the girls in the canteen? All the same, she answered him readily enough.

'Sarah? She left us, let me see, about three weeks ago. A good worker, too; I was sorry to see her go, sir.'

He thanked her pleasantly and went back to his car, then made the slow journey through the rush-hour traffic to Clapham Common. It was still early morning; if Sarah was at home he would have no compunction in getting her out of her bed. For all he knew she might be on the point of leaving.

The house, when he reached it, looked forlorn, and as he waited for someone to answer his knock he noticed that the downstairs windows lacked curtains. But someone was there; he heard footsteps in the hall and a moment later Mrs Twist opened the door.

'Lor' bless me, sir, and here was me thinking I'd never see you again.'

She stood aside for him to go in and he saw that the hall carpet had been taken up and that there were pale squares on the walls where the pictures had hung.

'Sarah has gone to Bournemouth, Mrs Twist?'

'No, sir, and never meant to. 'Ad a bit of a do with her ma, told 'er she'd got a good job here and meant to stay.' Mrs Twist snorted. 'Good job—she's working part-time at the supermarket in the High Street, filling shelves. Goes in the morning early and finishes at midday. And what she'll do in a week's time when the new owners move in, I don't know.'

Mr ter Breukel frowned. 'She told me she was going to live with her mother and stepfather... Where is this supermarket?'

'Go left at the end of the road and then take the second turning on the right; that'll bring you to it. There's a car park.'

He smiled suddenly. 'We shall be back shortly, Mrs Twist...'

Mrs Twist's nose twitched at the scent of romance. '*We*, sir?'

'Yes, Mrs Twist.'

The supermarket was crowded with shoppers. Mr ter Breukel found an assistant and asked to be taken to the Manager. Presently he found himself in a small crowded office with a harassed-looking man at the desk.

'If I might have a word,' began Mr ter Breukel, assuming what could only be described as his best bedside manner. Ten minutes later they left the office together, threading their way to the back of the place where the manager opened a door and invited him to go in.

'Will you need to see Miss Beckwith again?' asked Mr ter Breukel.

'No, there's no need. This is all very unusual, but in the circumstances…'

They shook hands, and Mr ter Breukel went in and shut the door behind him. Sarah was unpacking tomato soup, stacking the tins on a small trolley. She didn't turn round when she heard the door close.

'This is the last lot, when you're ready.'

She turned round then, and saw him. It was as though someone had lighted her pale face with a soft glow, and he allowed himself a huge sigh of relief.

'Oh,' said Sarah, 'how did you get here? Who told you? Why are you here anyway?'

He said with commendable calm, 'Hello, Sarah. I came in my car. Mrs Twist told me where to find you, and I've come to take you home.'

She said in a shaky voice, 'Well, I can't come yet. It's only half past ten.'

'You've resigned. I have seen the manager; you're free to leave now.'

Her mouth fell open. 'Resigned? But I've only been here a week, and I need a job.'

'No, you don't. But let us not stand here arguing. If you will get your coat I'll drive you back, then we can talk.'

'What about?'

'Us.'

She could see that there would be no arguing about it. Meekly she took off her overall, found her coat and went with him to his car. They drove the short distance without saying a word. Sarah felt as though she had been hit on the head and had become delirious, while he was perfectly calm and relaxed.

Mrs Twist made coffee and they sat in the kitchen, the only room in the house that still held any comfort. Mr ter Breukel ate all the biscuits, since he had missed his breakfast, and listened sympathetically to Mrs Twist's problems until Sarah, unable to sit there any longer wondering what was to happen next, murmured something about packing the china. All non-sense, of course, but it got her out of the room.

Mr ter Breukel paused long enough to thank Mrs Twist for his coffee and went after her, to find her in the dining room at the back of the house, which was now quite empty, smelling slightly of damp and emptiness. He shut the door after him and crossed the bare boards, and turned her round to face him.

'Before we say anything else, let us get one thing quite clear. I love you, Sarah, and I want to marry you. And if you would just throw your odd notions out of the window and learn to love me a little, I believe that we will be extremely happy together.'

He put his arms around her and pulled her close. 'I fell in love with you when I saw you first. I've told you that, but I'll tell you again...'

'You didn't tell me that you loved me.'

'No, I wanted you to be free to choose.' He kissed the top of her head. 'You told me that you were going to Bournemouth, and I thought you had chosen.'

'I didn't know you loved me, did I? Oh, Litrik, I love you too, only I've been so silly.'

'My darling girl, never that. At cross purposes, perhaps.' He wrapped her even closer and began to kiss her...

Presently, Sarah asked, 'How long will you be here in London?'

'A week only. You can stay here? No, that's unthinkable.' He thought for a moment, then kissed her once more. 'I have it. I have a little house in a village in Somerset; you shall go there, and Mrs Twist shall go with you if she would like that. We can be married there—the church is small and beautiful. I'll ask Suzanne to come over and keep you company. I'll have to go back to Arnhem for a couple of days, but I'll get a special licence and we'll marry the moment I come back.'

Sarah said, 'I haven't anything to wear.'

'That's easily dealt with. Am I going too fast for you, my dearest?'

'Yes, but I rather like it.' She stretched up to kiss him, to lend weight to her words. 'Of course there are all kinds of problems. Mother…?'

'We'll drive down and tell her. I'm free on Sunday.'

'She'll be angry.'

'I'll be with you, darling.'

They went out to lunch then, taking Mrs Twist with them, who was thrilled to bits at the idea of the wedding and equally delighted to go with Sarah to Somerset.

By the end of the meal Litrik had everything arranged. He would take her and Mrs Twist straight from Bournemouth to his country home, they would see the rector, and there would be no need for Sarah to return to London. And as for Mrs Twist, she had no doubt that she could get a nephew to mind the house while she was away. He left after lunch, and Sarah went back to the house with Mrs Twist and sat in the kitchen, wrapped in dreams.

It all went exactly as planned. Her mother had been angry, and then peevish, and Sarah, with Litrik beside her, had listened a little sadly, for it was apparent that her mother regarded her as an unpaid companion who would have to be replaced. Whatever Litrik had had to say to her stepfather had been brief. He'd refused to come to their wedding, but when Litrik had suggested that he would send a car to take her mother to ceremony, she'd agreed to go. 'I hope it's a decent affair,' she'd said, 'and not some hole-and-corner ceremony.'

They had left then, and driven up to Somerset to the small village where Litrik had his house. A nice, solid old house, not too large, with a lovely garden and open country at its back. He had a housekeeper there, a widow lady who lived in the village. She had opened the door to them with a warm smile, and a moment later a door had opened and Suzanne had rushed to meet them.

'I'm here until the wedding. It's Litrik's idea; I hope you're glad. We're going shopping...'

Litrik had left them then, and driven back to London. That evening he'd made a number of phone calls. After all, what were old friends for? Everything had gone according to plan. The rector had been helpful, the business of getting the licence was well in hand.

Litrik slept the sleep of a contented man, emptied his head of everything but his work each day, and only each evening did he phone Sarah.

Sarah got up early on her wedding day, and went to look out of the window. It was going to be good weather: blue sky and warm sunshine. And Litrik would be coming. The week had been restful and pleasant, for Suzanne was a good companion. They had shopped, and Suzanne had insisted on buying a white dress and a little veil. It was a very simple dress, but it suited her, and presently she went to her room to put it on. She was still in her dressing gown when Litrik knocked and came in.

He caught her close and kissed her. 'Mrs Twist is shocked. I'm not supposed to see you until we meet at church.' He took two cases from a pocket. 'There has been no time. We'll have to be engaged for an hour or so.' He slipped a sapphire and diamond ring on her finger and then opened the other case, saying, 'Pearls for my bride.'

He saw the tears in her eyes. 'My darling, don't cry.'

'I'm not. I'm just so happy.' She smiled then. 'Litrik, I don't know anything—will someone give me away? And where are we going afterwards, or may we stay here? And will the church be empty?'

He stooped to kiss her once more. 'Dr Benson is giving you away.'

He had gone again before she could ask any more questions. 'It's all topsy-turvy,' she told her reflection in the mirror as she arranged her veil just so. 'The bride's mother usually does everything and the bridegroom just turns up.'

Presently she found herself in the church porch, a bouquet of white roses in her hand and Dr Benson beside her. When they entered the church it wasn't empty at all. There was her mother, in a magnificent hat, there was Mrs Twist and Litrik's housekeeper, and there was Suzanne and the nice Professor Smythe. There were others too, friends of Litrik, she supposed, and people from the village.

She was suddenly so happy that she wanted to sing and dance, only of course she couldn't, not in this beautiful little church, with the organ playing softly and the rector waiting to marry them. And Litrik, dear Litrik, turning to look at her as she reached his side, a look so full of love that she caught her breath.

The rector began, 'Dearly beloved...' And Sarah thought, Oh, how exactly right, and slipped her hand into Litrik's. She felt his firm clasp, knowing that his hand would always be there when she needed it. She looked at the rector then, and he saw that she, whom he had thought of as a rather plain girl, was beautiful.

Something Blue
Emma Goldrick

CHAPTER ONE

THE dirt road swung upward, around a cluster of maple trees, and out on to the flat meadow that was the boundary between Marne Tilson's small farm and the larger Smith acres, up at the top of the hill. Beyond the hill, the road meandered across the mountains into New York. Below her, the town of Peterboro clung to the shadows of the valley. The hot July sunshine made Marne's breathing difficult, and perspiration ran down her oval freckled face and off the tip of her sharp little nose. At five feet eight, Marne was a walker of no mean skill. She had tied her straw-blonde hair back at the base of her neck, to clear the deck, so to speak.

Miccimuc brook chattered in the far corner of the meadow, birthed by a natural spring, and then wandered east towards the city. The spring was surrounded by a grove of willows, pines and oaks, almost concealing a shady resting place for country children. On the county map the Miccimuc was called a river. Even the long-gone tribe of Mohicans would have laughed at that. The spring was also the daily gathering point of half the birds in the county.

There was something moving in the shadows. Marne caught her breath, vaulted over the low dry-stone wall, and took a couple of trotting steps into the shade.

Her ancient grey cat, Morgan, came up beside her as if this were a two-cat race, and sputtered a high-pitched *meoow* at her. Marne pulled herself to a full stop. 'Of course,' she muttered, 'why should we be in any hurry? Just because his niece Becky called, all excited, to tell me that Rob was home and wanted to meet me? Am I as big a fool as I seem to be? Four years since our divorce became final, he wants to meet me? Four years since I've seen him.' She slowed to a walk, twisting gently on the balls of her feet so that her dress swung back and forth, and her hips as well. She came to a halt at the edge of the wood, her grey-green eyes studying the shadows.

He was sitting on the edge of the granite rock that they had used for so many years as a meeting place. His fishing line was in the water, the little red and white bobbin bouncing in the rush of the current. He leaned forward and came up into a crouch, all the thin bones of him apparent to view. Marne's heart skipped a beat. He had always had this effect on her; a gangly half-fed man a few inches taller than herself. Warm brown hair that she loved to caress. A thin face that was marvellously fluid, expressing his every thought. Rob Smith. She had once been Mrs Rob Smith. The sharpness of remembrance bit into her heart.

Marne came to a full stop, nervously brushing down her simple sundress, checking the angle of her shoulder-straps. Somehow she had to make him see she was not the *kid* he once had called her. One more deep breath to settle her nerves. 'Oh, is that you, Rob?' Her usually sweet contralto seemed to squeak, even to her own ears.

He turned his head and scanned her slowly, from heel to halter, pausing there to check what there was of her figure. 'Marne? I didn't see you coming.'

What a fool I am, she told herself. For the first time in four years he comes home. He calls, I come. How's that for enlightened disinterest, Marne Tilson? If he says, 'Lie down here. I want to talk to you,' do I do as I'm told? Wasn't that one major reason why I divorced him, because he was a dictator? What in God's good name am I doing here?

'Hi, kid. Come sit with me for a while.' He patted the

space next to him, and casually brushed it off. She cocked her head, then spread her skirts and joined him.

'It's—a surprise to find you here. Have you caught anything?'

'Did we ever?' He grinned down at her, a lop-sided full-mouthed grin. Not the most handsome man in the world, she told herself, but he'll do for the ordinary run-of-the-mill girl. Like me, for example. If I were looking for a man. Which I am definitely not! His dark brown hair lay against his head perfectly even though he'd passed the big three-oh these days.

A little whimper rose in Marne's throat. Remember the times, so many, when he would lie here with his head in my lap and I would stroke that soft hair. God! What am I doing to myself? Find something casual to talk about!

He tugged at his line, then turned back to her again with that thoughtful scan. 'It's good to see you, little bit. I had thought to come by your house, but I didn't know if I'd be welcome. My mother would only tell me that you hadn't married again. Tell me, how's your grandmother?'

'She died two years ago. I'm living alone in the old house.'

He paused reflectively. 'A wonderful lady, your grandmother.'

'Funny, she used to say the same about you. I never could understand why.'

'There's a difference between being neighbours and being married,' he said. 'You sound bitter.'

'I should be all sweetness and light?' After all those slights, and finally after the videotape that had arrived on her doorstep. The tape showing Sylvia Burroughs and Marne's husband making passionate love on a sofa in somebody's living-room. Yeah, I should be—she whipped out a handkerchief and stanched the incipient tears.

'So you called me—and here I am. What do you want, Rob?'

'Hey, it was a friendly divorce, wasn't it? Uncontested? By mutual agreement? No-fault?'

'Yes, all of that.' Because you didn't dare to appear in court after your lawyer saw my tape, Rob Smith, she thought furiously. Incompatibility, no doubt about it, and Judge Hanron had granted the no-fault decree after only five minutes of the hearing. Five minutes, to dissolve a two-year marriage.

'So why meet you here?'

'Because we always did, little bit. Halfway between, a neutral meeting ground. I didn't dare come down to the house. Too scared, I guess.'

'Scared of me? Even if I did remarry or anything, you'd be welcome. As a neighbour. It *was* a friendly divorce, wasn't it? You know that. And nothing's happened to me. I'm just the same as I always was.' And *don't* call me 'little bit'!

'I'm not sure of the friendly divorce,' he said gloomily. 'Would you believe, a just-graduated lawyer, and I didn't know about no-fault divorces.' He turned his eyes to her, searching her face. She could see pain writhing across his. 'And I still don't know why.'

'Well,' she muttered, 'it's all behind us now. I'm surprised you've come home. I haven't changed much, Rob. You're still welcome in these parts. I don't love you as I once foolishly did, but we can still be friends. Friends don't change.'

'I believe you haven't. Cool, generous—and prettier than ever, Marne. I do believe you've grown up. And Becky tells me you're her school teacher.'

'Yes, I went back to Amherst for a teaching degree. That's a change.'

'It must have been some struggle, working and studying. Why wouldn't you take the money I offered?'

'I didn't want your damn money,' she snapped. 'I didn't want anything of yours!'

'Yes, I remember,' he said. His voice was rough and deep and caressing, and the shivers ran up and down her spine. And when his big warm hand dropped on to her bare shoulder he felt her quivering.

'Independent little cuss.'

'Of course,' she mumbled. 'But not so little. Don't call me that.' You don't know why I wanted a divorce? Lord, there seemed to be a hundred reasons. She shivered again. It's like the old saying, Rob. 'Wear something old, something new, something borrowed, and something blue.' A vow of fidelity. I did, and I was and you weren't!

'Here, now, we can't have you shivering like that.' He pulled her over to where her hip met his, and the warmth brought colour to her face. They both watched the little bobbin, moving around with the speed of the current. Her mind ached from the thought of it all.

'Morgan the opportunist,' he said after a time. 'She's down there waiting to see if I catch anything.'

'She's missed you, Rob. There's nobody else in the neighbourhood who fishes here.'

'Cupboard love,' he said, chuckling. 'And you, Marne?'

'Me?'

'You. Have you missed me?'

'Well, I wasn't all that interested in fishing.' She was blushing again, and praying that the wind would manoeuvre the tree branches above her so that he couldn't see. What a stupid thing to say! Tell him that you didn't follow him around all those years just because he was a wonderful fisherman! But her tongue was too tied down, and would not co-operate. Marne took another deep breath and lunged for another conversational bit.

'Your new wife, is she pretty?'

He turned her chin up so he could see her eyes. 'You must be the only girl in the county who doesn't know.'

'Doesn't know what?'

'Doesn't know that I never did marry again. The girl was—nice, and a lawyer too. But who wants to be married to *nice*? Yeah, she was pretty. On the outside, at least. Her father wanted the marriage, of all things, but I wasn't marrying *him*, and I *couldn't* marry her.'

'Why not?' Softly spoken, but with a tremolo, as if she was afraid to know the answer to her question.

'I'm not sure I can answer that,' he responded. His hand tightened on her shoulder, almost painfully. 'When you've had the best it's hard to accept second-best.'

His meaning went right over her head. 'Well, then, you had a lucky break,' Marne said indignantly. 'There are lots of women in the world who'd jump at the idea of marrying you.'

'Great. Just what I need. Name two.' He looked as if he meant it, his face all solemn, his voice coaxing, and those little devil-spots dancing in his dark eyes.

And now you're backed into a corner, Marne yelled at herself, if you really are hunting the man. He's changed in some way. Some almost indefinable way. He's not the big, overgrown, rash boy he used to be. He's—lord, I don't know, do I? Speak up. Say a name or two. The county is overrun with willing spinsters. But her mind closed down, and she could not get the right words out. Or any words, for that matter. Because, she told herself, the truth is that nobody could love Rob Smith except Marne Tilson.

'Cat got your tongue?'

'No, I was—thinking.'

'Names just don't pop up into your mind, I suppose.' And this time the sparkle was gone from his eyes, and the cheer from his cold, hard voice.

But, having committed herself, Marne was totally unable to skate off the thin ice, no matter how much she wanted to.

'It sure would be nice to come home and find a woman waiting for me,' he mused.

'Is that why you came home?'

'I—more or less. I wanted to talk to you and—damn you, cat, get away from there!'

Morgan, leaning dangerously over the water as Rob's fishing line dipped underwater, had swiped at the bobbin and the little fish suspended below it, and had fallen ingloriously into the stream.

The water was cold. Winter or summer, it was cold. Morgan screamed in rage, threshed around between the line and the bank, and squalled some more. The fish, hardly bigger than a goldfish, wiggled off the hook and was gone. Rob Smith was up and off the rock before Marne could gear herself up to move. He yelled too, as his shoes filled with the cold water. With one big hand he flipped the cat out of the water and a good five feet up the bank. And then, overbalanced, he lost his footing on the slippery rocks of the bed of the spring, teetered, and fell over.

The water in the middle of the pool came up to his armpits. Startled again, Marne stared, and then giggled. He was such a big man, and so pompous when he wanted to be, and the water came up to his—but of course, he's sitting down!

Morgan, still complaining, came over to her shoulder, seeking sympathy. She spared a hand to scratch behind the cat's ears. And out in the middle of the stream Rob stood up, legs apart, hands on hips, glaring.

'Funny, is it?' Years ago, had this sort of thing happened, Marne would have giggled, and then started running before he caught up to her. He was a great believer in killing the messenger, she remembered. But that was years ago. Lord knew what he'd do today. She swallowed the giggle and backed off up to the crest of the rock as he stomped out of the water.

'Funny?'

'Well, not exactly,' she temporised. He stretched a hand out in her direction, and, without thinking, she offered help. His hand was big and strong and—tempting? Somehow she didn't remember it being like that. So her guard was down as he gave a yank and she sailed by him head first and plunged into the pond.

Where the pool came only up to his mid-chest as he sat there, on Marne it was over her head. She came up, sputtering indignantly, only to be snatched up out of the water and conveyed effortlessly to dry land.

'You'll have to believe me, I really didn't intend to do that,' Rob said, Marne managed to get the hair out of her eyes and looked up at him. That devilish twinkle that she knew so well was sparking in his dark eyes. Nowhere could she find a smidgen of remorse. Nowhere.

'And I'm supposed to believe that? You might put me down!'

'When I'm good and ready,' he returned, losing the twinkle and transferring into a brooding presence bent over her. She wiggled half-heartedly. He let her slip slowly through his arms until her feet touched ground, and then backed away a step or two.

'My lord, I've been blind for years!'

'What?' A hesitant question. There was something in his eyes now that she had never seen before. Some hunting animal had taken over the gentle character of the boy she knew too well. And those feral eyes were travelling up and down her figure as if he had never seen it before.

Troubled, Marne looked down at herself. Her thin cotton dress was soaked, cling to her at every crevice and around every curve. Under the dress, because it was such a hot day, she wore nothing. Everything except her conscience was on display.

'Well, who have we here?' he murmured softly. 'Marne Tilson, all grown up?'

'I—yes,' she stammered. 'Whom. That's all of me there is.'

'What I see is what I get?'

'What the devil are you talking about, Rob Smith?' She stamped her foot indignantly and instantly regretted it. Granite rocks were the bones of the earth, and her foot complained at the abuse.

He reached out for her and drew her back into his arms, and for a moment they both dripped over each other. 'Here,' he offered gently, and before she could react he had pulled off his wet shirt and was towelling her hair.

One could hardly say he was drying her. His shirt was as wet as she. But he was doing something—something that warmed her, that sent little *frissons* down her spine and back again. She opened her eyes and looked up at him. Yes, there was no doubt, this was the Rob Smith she had known and—hated? No doubt at all. She groaned and dived back against his bare chest again. This was the man, but not the man. Or she was not the woman she had been, and, being unable to settle the difference, she took refuge in tears.

'Hey, none of that, little bit.'

'Don't you call me that,' she said, emphasising each word. 'I'm not a little bit. And I'm certainly not *your* little bit! Turn me loose before I—'

'Set your cat on me?' He laughed gently, but with her head against his chest it sounded like a roar. Filled with impotent rage, she finally remembered the pointed toes of her shoes, and swung one of them into his ankle.

He yelled, and danced around in a circle on one leg.

'Dammit, woman, don't do that,' he snapped. Marne managed to break away, and then added a step or two to the distance between them.

'Sweet little bit hell,' he muttered. 'More like a wild cat, lady.'

He moved towards her threateningly, but she was unable to move. With water still dripping off her dress, feet apart, ready for flight, she found herself unable to command her muscles to movement.

'What are you going to do?' A question asked in her quavering voice, a voice touched with considerable fear.

'First I'm going to take you out into the sunshine to dry off.' He offered her a nasty little stage-door leer. 'And then you'll find out.'

His arms were around her, pulling her against the steel of his chest, binding her helplessly to him by strength and hypnotism. She struggled weakly, to no avail, as her prison closed around her, and then his face blotted out the sun as he took dead aim at her lips and moved to contact.

It was not what she had expected. Just a touch of a kiss, and then when he moved away a sort of electric *snap*, as if lightning were flashing between them. She stopped struggling. His lips roved, down to her ear-lobes, back to her chin, around the base of her neck, across her bare shoulders, and gently down into the declivity between her breasts.

'Marne, Marne,' she heard him whisper. 'Why have I been such a damned blind fool?'

It's time, she told herself. Time to break out of this daze. Time to do *something* to escape the trap. But it required all her attention to find the right words. Every time his lips moved to a new target she lost control all over again.

It was Morgan who saved her. The old cat, neither willing nor able to share the limelight, grumbled at her a time or two, and then unfolded her claws halfway and took a free-swinging swat at Marne's ankle.

The sharp little pain was just enough. 'No,' she muttered as Rob's lips came down again. She managed to free one hand, but only had the strength to shove a finger between his lips and his target. He stopped.

'No?' As disbelieving as one could ever find in the male kingdom.

'No,' she repeated, now fully in control. 'I'm not your dinner. And I'm surely not your appetiser. Just because you need a woman, and I happen to be the only one within ten miles, I don't expect—'

'Boy, how far wrong can you be, woman?' he said as he held her out at arm's length. 'Listen up, Marne. We've been friends a long time?'

'Yes,' she said hesitantly, 'with some exceptions. I can't swear that it's all been peaches and cream.'

'But you'd be willing to do me a favour?'

'That all depends. What favour? How long?'

'About six months would do it,' he returned cautiously. 'Would you?'

'Would I what?'

He set her aside and paced back and forth for a moment. 'Marne, you know how hard it is to make it big in law these days. The woods are full of lawyers. I've been with a large firm down in Washington for three years now. And I'm not really getting anyplace.' He left it there.

Gurgling water and chirping birds took over. The engines of a high-flying plane broke the natural cycle of sound. Marne looked up at him. There was a do-or-die expression on his face. The wind fingered her hair, still heavy with wetness, and loaded with pine scent. Her dress, pressed against her by the same wind, outlined her lithe little figure. She shivered against the coolness of it. It *had* to be the wind against her wet dress. It couldn't be anything else, could it?

'There's a "but" in it, isn't there?' she asked softly.

He nodded his head.

'Well,' she said, sighing, 'lay it on me and then we'll see.'

His breath ran out of him in a massive sigh, almost as if he had been holding it in all this time. 'Thank God for you, Marne,' he said.

'Yes, sure, thank God for me,' she sighed. 'What do I have to do?'

'It won't be difficult.' His tone hardly belied his statement. 'I've decided to come home and go into politics. Ma isn't growing any younger. She and Becky both need someone to look after them. My brother Bill is well settled in Worcester. Our present sheriff, who is seventy years old, said that he won't run again in the September primary. So *I've* decided to run.'

'But...' She laid a hand over his mouth to stop him from talking. It was such a familiar thing to do that she gave it no thought for the moment. 'But—people say that the whole county government is as crooked as a snake's belly.'

He was smiling as he looked at her. 'That's why I want to run,' he said. 'A new broom sweeps clean, and all that sort of thing.'

'People say,' she continued in a half-whisper, 'that the only reason why anybody would run for a thirty-thousand-dollar-a-year job is because there's so much patronage attached to the office.'

'Do they say that? Isn't that one of America's age-old beliefs? "To the victor belong the spoils"?'

'That's—well, *I* don't care. It's *your* reputation that might suffer.'

'Then you'll help?'

Marne nodded, not daring to speak at the moment. After a moment she said, 'Yes, I'll help. With what?'

'The only real problem,' he said, 'is that this county is about as old-fashioned as it can get. So I need to find a...temporary wife—to display on the election platforms and at the women's clubs and—'

Deep silence. 'Marne?'

But Marne, having fought the good fight, lost control of her speeding little world. Oxygen was hard to come by. She collapsed, and if he hadn't grabbed her just in time she would have fallen into the brook again.

CHAPTER TWO

MARNE awoke the next morning in some sort of daze. She knew exactly where and what she was, but couldn't quite figure out the why of it all. Her head felt as if it were a balloon, and her nose was all stuffed up. Damn man, she thought, throwing me in the pool. Now I'll have a summer cold for the rest of the year! The sun was shining, mountain-high, through the dusty windowpanes in her bedroom. And someone knocked on her door.

Hers was an old ranch-style home, built all on one floor because Great-Grandpa had hardly been able to climb stairs. 'Come in. Don't stand out there abusing my door,' she yelled. She felt the need to shout, but her ears hurt the minute she did. The hinge on the screen door sounded off, footsteps pattered across her living-room, and Becky walked into her bedroom.

'My goodness!' The little girl came over and jumped up on to the foot of the bed. Her long blonde almost-white hair fell behind her back to her hips. The old mattress bounced; Marne moaned.

'I have a cold in my nose and an ache in my head. And it's none of your darn business,' Marne snapped. 'That— damn uncle of yours. He ought to be horsewhipped! Hand me that tissue box.'

'He came home late too,' Becky said primly. 'And he's been roaming around the house like a black bear. Even Ma can't stand him. She went out to do the eggs. I thought I'd just run over here and—you're not really mad at me, Marne?'

'No, I'm not mad at you, love,' Marne returned. 'I've

only contracted the biggest cold in the county. I haven't
had a bit to drink. But I can just see your uncle laying it
on. Bolstering his courage, was he?'

'I just don't know what to make of it,' Becky said.
'There's something going on in our house, and I just don't
know what it is!'

'Well, you can't always guess right, Sherlock Holmes.
Of course we weren't drinking together. You know darn
well I haven't touched a drop in seven years. No, I came
straight home after he pushed me into the—I came straight
home.'

'And you were mad as a wet hen? Or just wet?' A spec-
ulative pause by a very sharp little lady. 'He was, too.
Soaking wet. Claimed you pushed him into the brook.' The
attentive little head cocked itself slightly and Becky peered
into her eyes.

'Well, not the first time,' Marne admitted cautiously.
'What a fine fellow you have for an uncle. Picking on a
nice—person—like me. Throwing me in the water and all,
and then—'

'And then?' The sharp little eyes dug deeper into hers.
Marne took a deep breath. The only thing she knew for
sure about Becky was that everything the child heard was
immediately re-broadcast throughout the town. Up hill and
down dale, so to speak.

'And then nothing,' Marne said stiffly. 'Did your uncle
send you over to spy on me this morning?'

'Nope. He was just getting dressed when I left the house.
But I'm sure he will be along soon. The only thing he said
to Ma last night was that he had hope. Well, "it's a good
idea, and there's a little hope" was what he said.' The child
came to a stop. 'Why, you don't even have no nightgown
on, Marne.' Another silence. 'Hope for what?'

'How would I know?' Marne said desperately. 'And if
your uncle comes over here this mornng I'll probably kill

him. Now, if you would kindly get out of my bedroom I could get dressed!'

'Marne?' The little girl hesitated, showing a trace of tears in her eyes. 'Did you ever think of getting married again?'

'Yes, I've thought about it from time to time,' Marne admitted. 'There were one or two men in the area—but that didn't work out.'

'Oh, no!' The child's face fell. 'No, you can't marry nobody else. You gotta marry Rob again. I need an aunt, Marne, and you were the nicest aunt a girl ever had and that's why you can't marry nobody else.' All said ruefully and in a rush as she slid off the bed. 'I'll wait on the porch for you?'

'No, I don't think so,' Marne told the child regretfully. 'I have my exercises to do, and then I've got a day full of heavy thinking. You'd better run along home, love. I'll see you tomorrow, shall I? And I'm pleased, love, that I was such a successful aunt. Who knows? Some day a fine girl might come down the Pike and marry your uncle and be the best aunt in the world for you. Scoot now.'

'Nobody's gonna do that. Unless it's you, Marne. And if I ever see anyone else coming down the Pike and looking at Rob I'll kill her. Or set a snake in her bed! Are you gonna do your exercises before you get dressed?'

'Yes, I am,' Marne said. 'Don't I always? What have you been doing, peeking in my windows?'

'Not me,' Becky defended herself stoutly. 'But there are those who would, you know. All right, all right, I'm going. Maybe you'll feel better tomorrow!'

Marne watched the stiff little back march straight out of the door and down the steps. 'It's hardly possible that I'll feel better in the next month. Get up,' she ordered herself, and managed to get a bare foot on the floor. 'What a child. I wonder what it would be like to be her mother?' She stood up to look out of the window, but Becky was already at the curve in the path. Marne shrugged her shoulders, and began the slow stretching exercises that made up the first five minutes of her morning ritual, so that she could hardly follow Becky any further.

That little miss came to a stop in the middle of the path as her favourite uncle came along. He was smiling; in fact he was looking almost human. The little posy of wild flowers in his hand gave away his intentions.

Becky looked her uncle over very carefully, biting on her lip. 'I did something wrong?' he asked.

'No, everything's just fine. I was thinking. Marne's doing her exercises. She says for you to just come right in.' Little Becky was two hundred feet further away, a very self-satisfied smile on her face, when she heard the initial wild scream of anger from the house behind her. Her uncle Rob, she reminded herself, was always the slow one, and needed help.

'Look,' Rob said in his best placating voice. 'I swear my little niece said I was to just walk right in. Need some help with that towel?'

'You come within two feet of me, Mr Smith, and they'll be scraping you off the wall.' The only thing Marne could find when Rob Smith walked into the house in the midst of her nude aerobic exercises was the small hand towel that she normally kept over the kitchen sink. Marne was a good-sized girl; the towel was no match for her. And the more she tugged at the towel the wider that grin on his face became.

'What are you grinning at? You look like an expectant baboon!' The words exploded out of her from an empty mind. Every thought had evaporated in that moment when his hand had settled on her bare shoulder.

'Thank you,' he said mildly. 'But if you want my advice

I recommend you pull the towel a little lower. There's a great deal of you uncovered in that direction.'

'Yes, I'll bet there is,' she snarled. 'And if I move the towel a little lower I'll be on display even— oh— Hell! Look, Mr Smith, why don't you just go out on the porch while I finish dressing? Isn't that a reasonable idea?'

'Not from the male point of view,' he said, chuckling. 'There's always a certain amount of viewing that improves the world. Now, Marne—your towel is slipping!'

'I'm going to bash you to a fare-thee-well,' she muttered as she abandoned the towel. 'I want to show you something else I've learned.'

'No, now, don't slap my face,' he said, chuckling. Marne moved forward, trying not to slap his face, but to get a good hold on him, and throw him over her shoulder in the manner of instruction in her martial-arts class.

Unfortunately, when Marne took that martial arts course she had received an 'A' for enthusiasm, and an 'F' for co-ordination. In this case she stamped her foot to get a good purchase on the kitchen linoleum, and forgot that she had just waxed that floor the day before. Her foot moved out from under her, and she slid across the room like a bowling ball, with Rob the pin. Together they rumbled across the kitchen and smashed against the wall, Marne on top.

'Well, now,' Rob said as he gathered up this armful of nude woman sitting on top of him, 'look what I have here!'

'Don't you dare laugh!' Marne could hardly move. Just how, she asked herself, did Lady Godiva maintain her cool?

'I wouldn't dare laugh,' he said. She struggled against his 'helping hand', wiggling for all she was worth. But finally she broke free, scrambled across the floor and ran for her room. When she came back out, wearing her old robe, he was still sitting on the floor against the wall, holding the back of his head.

'Help me up?' He was a true penitent, and looked contrite enough, and she could hardly forget that once she had loved him. So she walked over, helped him up, and, walking in a three-legged parade, they moved out on to the porch, where he sank gratefully on to the swing.

'Better?' she asked.

'I guess. I bumped my head on the wall.'

'I hope that teaches you a darn lesson. I know Tae kwon do.'

He held up a hand in surrender. 'Which you just happened to study while I've been gone?'

'That's right. Oh, dear. You *did* hurt your head! I'll bring you an ice-pack.'

'Yeah,' he muttered. 'Ice-pack.' And then he managed a little smile. 'You know something, Marne?' She cocked her head at him. 'Bruises and ice-pack and all, it was worth it!'

'I'll bet it was.' His eyes followed her as she walked slowly back into her bedroom. Something gentle, she told herself as she thumbed through her meagre wardrobe. Something demure? But the only thing she could come up with was one of her teaching uniforms. Well, not exactly a uniform, just one of several look-alike black skirts and white blouses which fitted loosely, contained plenty of pockets for pencils and notes, and did nothing to stir up the male teachers. But she did add a little mascara, a touch of purple eyeshadow, and a gloss of pale Temptation for her lips. When she came back outside he was almost himself, up on his feet, with a hand on the banister to balance, looking down into the valley and the city below. She almost forgot the ice-pack, and had to go back for it.

'Ah, you're ready,' he commented. 'I remember that. Always on time, you were.'

And if that's all you remember about me, Marne fumed to herself, you hardly know a single thing about me! He leaned on the rail, then marched back to the swing.

'How about it?' he asked. 'Have you given any thought to our marrying?'

'Just to do you a favour?'

'Just to do me a favour.'

'Why don't we just *say* we've been remarried, and act it out from there?' she suggested. 'You were always a great actor. I'm sure I could keep up. It would be simple.'

'It would be simple,' he acknowledged, 'but if the word got out I'd be thrown out of the election campaign. People will vote for many strange people, Marne, but they won't vote for a proven liar. Besides, my mother would know, and I'd hate to have her down at the church praying for us every day. I couldn't stand it.'

'That's a big load you're placing on my shoulders,' she told him. 'I don't know. If we had another wedding ceremony we'd be lying to God. That's a terrible responsibility.'

'That too. But there are millions of people who get married without love.'

'Perhaps. And without consummation? I couldn't allow that.'

'You drive a hard bargain,' he groaned, but she could see it was artificial. 'You don't believe in recreational sex?'

'No, I don't. And let me tell you one more thing, Rob Smith. If you get me tied up in just one more lie or deceit, I'm out of here. No arguments, no explanations, I'm just gone!'

He shook his head, gently because it still ached. 'You *do* drive a hard bargain,' he said dolefully.

'There are always more women in the valley you could take up with.'

'No. That won't do. I have to have you and your name. After all, your grandfather and father were the finest doctors in the county. Everybody knew Doc Tilson. Well, how about it?'

'I have to think,' she said, and walked back into the kitchen.

'Take your time,' he called after her.

Marne slumped at the kitchen table and rested her head between her hands. What to do? Make a summary of all those things that went wrong in their first marriage? Or admit without question that she still loved him, and probably would for the rest of her life, no matter *what* he did? And in the meantime, being married again would allow her to be close to him, to snap up any crumbs he might cast in her direction. And—what the devil am I doing?

From outside she heard him call to her cat. 'Come sit with me, Morgan?'

Marne's anger sputtered to a stop. Her hands stilled. Her blouse was only half buttoned, but she ignored it. Her mind was busy again.

What's the matter with me? she asked herself. I don't like the man. I didn't like him when he was a teasing damn boy, and now he's grown bigger and there's more of him for me not to like. So why am I all over shivers when he touches me, and why am I debating this silly proposal?

Why? I've been kissed by practically every male of my age in the town during the past four years, and never had such a response as I get from Rob. So he kissed me—on my nose, no less—and I'm already turned on up to the halfway point. If he *really* kissed me, what would it be like?

'Don't be too long in there,' he called from out on the porch. 'Morgan's getting restless. Your porch swing needs a coat of paint.'

Paint—paint, Marne raged to herself. I'm going to get dressed again, enough to knock your eye out, Rob Smith, and then I'm going to come out there and paint all over you, you rotten, scheming—neighbour. And *that* seemed like such a practical thing to do that she went ahead and did it.

The fashions had changed, of course, but from her early seventeens she resurrected a pair of boys' trousers, with silver buckles just under the knees, a plain boyish shirt tucked into the waistband, and a leather belt with a large silver buckle.

Rob was waiting for her on the porch. He patted the swing next to him as an invitation. Remembering the scene by the stone just one day earlier, which had ended up with her being thrown into the pool, Marne shook her head at him, folded her hands behind her, and kept her distance.

'My, aren't we charming?' He stood up, still cuddling Morgan in one arm.

'Yes, we are, aren't we?' she shot back. She reached up and undid the top button of the shirt. Rob's eyes followed her fingers as if glued to them.

'And while you're at it please stop trying to seduce my cat. She's a good old cat, and we care for each other.'

'I have no intention of seducing your cat,' he said as he leaned over and dropped Morgan to the floor. The cat protested momentarily, then sneered at them both and stalked off. 'I'm saving all my poor talents to seduce the cat's owner.'

'Don't think you can talk me into anything with that smooth talk,' she snapped.

'Why are you blushing, Marne?'

'None of your business. Why ever did you come back here after all those years? We've all just about gotten you out of our hair.'

'I told you yesterday,' he said softly. 'I came to see how you had grown up.'

Marne stirred uneasily. He made it sound so simple, so truthful, that she almost believed, even if she knew he was lying. It took an effort for her to respond. 'Now that's a crock of worms, Robert Smith. You probably didn't even remember my name until your mother reminded you!' It was a shot in the dark, but she scored a hit, and now it was his turn to blush. Not in her manner. Marne's skin was ivory; when she blushed it turned red. His skin was always a dark tan; his blush merely turned his face darker than normal. He laughed, trying unsuccessfully to brush it off.

'You never used to be such a sceptic,' he drawled.

'Sucker, you mean.'

'Never that. Look, Marne, I need you. At least sit down with me and talk it out.'

'Talk,' she charged him. 'Just talk.' And then, because all her interior had always been marshmallow, she gestured towards the door. 'Come into the kitchen. I'll make some coffee—and I'll listen. Maybe I misheard you yesterday. Coming?'

'I wouldn't miss it for all the tea in China,' he said as he took control of the door and shepherded her inside. 'I've been to China,' he continued as she ground the beans and set the pot to steep. 'Fine place. But all the tea is really in India. Ever been to India, Marne? We could go—together—after the election.'

He sat down at the table without invitation. She slapped a mug down in front of him and reached for the pot. 'You know darn well I've never been out of Massachusetts,' she grumbled as she poured the steaming liquid. He hitched his chair an inch or two away from the steam—just in case, Marne told herself, and was unable to restrain a giggle. The big brave man!

'Well?' She poured her own cup a little more daintily, stirred in a sugar cube, and sat down opposite him. He looked so—familiar, there across the table from her. So—masculine and dependable. And if I keep thinking about him along those lines he'll have me dancing the hula in his bedroom almost any day now, she thought. 'Well?' she repeated.

'It's a detailed story,' he said. He was watching her like a hawk, while his two hands cherished his coffee-mug.

'So the quicker you begin, the sooner you'll end,' she said primly.

'Hey,' he said, protesting. 'But, if that's the way it's to be, you'll get it, bare bones and all.' He readjusted his chair, took a nervous sip of his black coffee, and told her the entire story.

'There's one born every minute,' Marne said. He looked up at her, scowling. 'P.T. Barnum,' she added. '"There's a sucker born every minute." So now you're going to tell me that you need money to keep the wolf from your mother's door—'

'And Becky's too,' he added. 'You like Becky.'

'Damn you, that's blackmail!'

'Well, I never said it would be easy.'

'I like your mother, too.'

'That's good. She likes you.'

'And if you get this—political office?'

'County sheriff.' His eyes lit up and he smacked his lips as if already tasting the victory. 'The election will be tough, but there's no incumbent. I think everything will work out fine. Especially with your name up on the banners. People still remember the Tilson name. Your father was the finest doctor the county ever had.'

'My name on the advertising?'

'You bet. Local boy marries local girl. It'll be a cake-walk. Takes a little time, of course, but we can do it. You and I.'

'Takes a little time? You and I?' A pregnant pause. 'You said in six months, yesterday.' Her eyes challenged him.

'I was only guessing. Perhaps six months will do it. I can only try.' His big dark eyes gave her one of his patented trust-me looks. Marne remembered vaguely how many times she had looked into those eyes and dived in head first. His mother in trouble? Becky? Six months?

'We are going to let everybody think we're still married?'

'Oh, no. We'll have to have another ceremony. Nothing fancy, of course. Just a little get-together at my place.'

'Now just slow down,' she snapped. 'This is going to be a fake marriage, of course?'

'Well—of course,' he agreed. His eyes lit up at the obvious surrender. 'A marriage of convenience, so to speak. But there has to be a wedding and all that. It has to be a well-constructed farce, right?'

'No hanky-panky,' she snapped.

'No— Oh. There has to be a certain amount of hugging and kissing,' he insisted.

'But it all ends just outside the bedroom door,' she insisted.

'Marne, I guarantee that this wedding will be just what you want it to be. Is that satisfactory?'

Marne slammed her chair back and paced up and down the room. Morgan called to be let in. Marne opened the screen door and then let it slam shut behind her cat. My cat has good taste, she told herself. What shall I do, Morgan?

Her cat marched straight across the room, sniffed at the bottom of Rob's trousers, then vaulted up into his lap, curled herself up, and closed her eyes. It seemed to be some sort of omen.

'I can't believe I'm even listening to this,' she said softly. 'Nobody with any sense would enter into this kind of proposal. You want me to—to marry you just so you can present a false appearance to the voters?'

'I'd not be doing anything that any other politician wouldn't do,' he said, aggrieved. 'It isn't as if I were planning to rob the state treasury, you know. Like most politicians, I expect to be honest most of the time.'

'But I don't even like you,' Marne wailed. 'I can't forget the thousand and one things that led to our divorce! They left me with a bad taste in my mouth.'

'I think that's an advantage,' he said. 'If you don't like me there's no possible reason why the marriage would turn into something permanent. Besides, it will be a change for you—get you out of the boredom of school teaching, and make some money on the side. I'll pay you for your services, of course.'

'Who?' Marne snapped. 'Who told you about my being bored with school teaching? Who? Oh, God, that rotten little blabbermouth niece of yours.'

'That's right.' He nodded sagely; there was a Cheshire-cat smile on his face.

I really ought to hit him, Marne told herself. Give him a good bash right across that Roman nose of his, and roll him down the hill into the lake. But—there ought to be *some* adventure in a girl's life. The whole story sounds as if it's fresh out of a fairy-tale, but what else is there? Another summer of odd jobs, then back to the school again? Lord, what wonderful choices I have! Remember when I used to like him? Maybe if I worked at it we might come to that again. So flip a coin. Morgan likes him. Becky loves him—most of the people I know thoroughly approve of him. So why shouldn't I take a six-month chance on him?

'You don't need to pay me,' she sighed. 'I wouldn't take your money as alimony, and…' A long, gusty sigh. 'All right. I'll give it a try.' Said softly as she watched her cat's head bob up and down. And then, much louder, 'If it doesn't work out the way you say, I'm going to get a quick annulment and leave you holding the baby. You hear, Rob Smith?'

'Oh, I hear,' he said. There was a very large self-satisfied smile on his face. 'Now we'd better go up the hill and tell my mother. She told me at breakfast that you were too sensible to fall for a story like mine.'

The Smith house was a good half-mile up the hill. Bigger than Marne's, it was a typical rambling New England farmhouse, with additions at odd corners, and a look of smartness and new paint about it. Rob's mother Mabel waited at the door. Becky hid behind her, clutching at her hand. Mrs Smith was a roly-poly widow of fifty-five, who had watched over Marne from a distance until after her grandmother died, and then moved more actively into her guardianship.

'Don't ever tell me,' Mabel Smith said as she raised both hands up beside her cheeks in astonishment. 'She agreed?'

'Of course,' her younger son said. 'Did you ever have a doubt about my powers of persuasion?'

'More than once,' his widowed mother returned sarcastically. 'Are you sure he didn't just sweet-talk you into this, Marne?'

'I—well, I guess he did,' Marne said reflectively. 'But isn't that always the way?' Mrs Smith led the way into the parlour and raised the curtains. Marne paid it all no mind; it was the sort of thing one did in old New England houses. The parlour was always reserved for formal functions— weddings, funerals, the curate's formal house calls. And in between times the curtains were kept lowered to keep the rugs and furnishings from fading.

'Set yourself down.' Mrs Smith gestured towards the couch. 'And you two,' turning to her orphaned grandchild. 'Get out to the kitchen and make some coffee. Marne and I have some talking to do.'

'Now, then,' the older woman bustled for a moment, sat down in the chair opposite, and gave a sigh, 'I had always hoped—' she said. 'But then that shark swam up and tried to swallow him and—well, no matter. You really mean to go through with it all, Marne?'

It was almost as if she were holding the escape hatch open for Marne to have one last chance to get out of it.

'I—said I would,' Marne said, almost whispering. 'I'm a little frightened by it all, but I'll just grit my teeth and go through with it. You would rather I didn't? What shark was that?'

'Lord, child. You're just what the man needs. A farm girl who'll keep him in line. As for the shark, she was a lovely lady who used to live in these parts.'

'Not exactly a farm girl. Peterboro has almost seventy-five-thousand residents. I only wish...' Marne said. 'I can't remember. It was all so sweet and romantic, and then everything fell to pieces. I was too angry to think, and too young to know, and so I dropped him like a hot coal. Poor Rob. And now he feels that he did nothing wrong—and I don't have the courage to tell him.'

'There's no hurry,' Mother Smith replied with her warmest smile. 'You'll have years of time together to sort everything out. The wedding is certainly not going to be so quick that—'

'Hey, are you two already talking wedding?' Rob Smith interrupted as he walked into the room carrying a tray of coffee. Becky pranced behind him, carrying sugar and milk.

'Yes,' his mother replied, smiling. 'The bride's family always takes care of the wedding, but Marne doesn't have a family. So it's up to us to help her out. I thought perhaps—September?'

'Ha!' Her son set the tray down carefully and poured the drinks. As he handed out the mugs he continued. 'The election is in November,' he said. 'I need to have Marne aboard for the campaign. How about—a week from Tuesday?'

'Good lord,' his mother sighed. 'This isn't going to be

something conducted by a justice of the peace? It takes a little time to get a wedding together.'

'I'm going to be the bridesmaid,' Becky said.

'Hush. We have some important things to settle. Bridesmaids can wait. Marne, what do you have to say to that? A wedding a week on Tuesday?'

Marne looked at them all, staring back at her as if she knew what was going on. 'A week on Tuesday, or two weeks, or a month? I don't care. I haven't the slightest idea how it should come about. Grandma took charge of everything when we—the first time. I just sort of stood around, trying to look important.'

'Then that's settled,' Rob chimed in.

'At that rate we'd better have the ceremony at home,' his mother said.

'And the Reverend Mr Hunter could perform it,' Rob added. 'He's retired now, and wishes he wasn't. A nice wedding service would be just the thing to get his mind out of the doldrums.'

'And I can be the bridesmaid,' Becky repeated anxiously.

'And Betsy Willard to play the organ,' Mrs Smith inserted.

'If it's working,' Rob said. 'I'll get it overhauled.'

'And we'll hire a caterer for afters,' Mrs Smith said. 'Parties are great, but I'm tired of doing all that clearing up afterward.'

The Smiths looked at each other and smiled. Everything seemed to be working out just right.

'But—but what do *I* do?' Marne whispered. The room fell silent.

'Oh, my,' Mrs Smith said as she leaned forward to take one of Marne's hands.

'All you have to do is look beautiful,' Rob said as he took the other. 'Look beautiful, be on time—'

'And we must get you a wedding gown.' That from Mrs Smith.

'I—really can't afford it,' Marne said. There was a little trickle of salt water running down from her left eye, and her nose was running.

'Not to worry,' Rob told her. 'I'll have to get a loan to finance the whole thing, and we'll just add the wedding dress on to the list. Right?'

'Right,' Becky cheered.

'That girl has a terrible cold,' Mrs Smith said. 'Bed and hot lemonade for her. What ever happened to you, my poor dear?'

'Rob threw her into the creek,' Becky commented. Every other person in the group glared at her. The child shrugged her shoulders and threw back that long blonde mane of hers.

Marne looked slowly around the little planning group. Busy planning my life away, she told herself glumly. Is this *really* going to be right? But all those smiles, and the dreams behind them, stiffened her backbone. After all, it was only for six months. What could go wrong in six months? Plenty. She shuddered again, not knowing whether to laugh or to cry.

'But you don't think you'd prefer to marry some other woman, Rob?'

All the smiles disappeared. The meeting began to look like a funeral directors' convention. It was too much to bear. 'All right,' Marne stammered into the silence. 'It will be fine. It will be—right!'

CHAPTER THREE

TUESDAY week came up roses. The sun popped up early and bright, and light cool winds were blowing across the Berkshires from New York State. 'God's in his heaven,' Marne Tilson told herself. 'And I've almost gotten over the sniffles. So why am I so depressed?'

'We all have those moments.' Mrs Smith was hovering at her side, making final adjustments to the three-quarter-length ivory dress. The slim gown clung to her bodice, marched down firmly to her hips, and then flared out and down to mid-calf. A high lace collar clung to her neck, with a sheer silk transparent panel that covered, but actually left on view, her shoulders and the upper curves of her breasts. Long sleeves, with pearls sewn into the cuffs, came down her slender arms to almost an inch above her wrists. Altogether a dainty thing that revealed a little and promised much.

When we first married it was in the congregational church, Marne thought. I wore my grandmother's pristine white gown, designed in the Edwardian tradition, with a trailing veil that almost blinded me. Grandpapa walked me down the aisle, and four of my high-school girlfriends served as bridesmaids. Lord knows which of us was the most shaken. The veil was a marvel; it hid the fact that I cried all the way down the aisle. Well, I won't cry this time. Not a tear!

'Are you sure you wouldn't want my mother's veil?' Marne shook her head. She wanted no more blinding veils. Both at that first ceremony, and for a year afterwards, she had been blinded by love.

'No. Just the flowers.'

Mrs Smith carefully fitted the little coronet of flowers on top of Marne's straw-blonde hair. 'It does look—fragilely delicious.'

Marne mumbled an affirmative. She knew everything and nothing. In twenty minutes all the guests would have arrived, and she would be expected to walk down the stairs, smile at everyone, and walk up to the improvised altar. Where *he* would be waiting. She could hear the splatter of conversation floating up the stairs. Women's voices, all the teachers from the elementary school where Marne had worked for three years. All punctuated by a few deep male voices. Rob and his brother Bill, who would be his best man. Mr Dixon, the school principal, who had volunteered to give her away. The Reverend Mr Josias Hunter, dressed in his best, whose once-deep voice had begun to crack after sixty years of serving the methodist church. All waiting for the *pièce de résistance*, Marne Tilson.

There was bird song echoing in at the window, and the smell of charcoal being lit for the feast to follow. In the far distance a labouring freight locomotive could be heard, working its way through the pass that led to New York State.

'Nervous?' Mrs Smith asked. There was a great deal of understanding in her voice, a touch of sympathy every time her fingers caressed the gown. 'Bridal jitters?'

'I guess so,' Marne responded. Her teeth were chattering, and an occasional shiver ran up and down her spine. 'If I'm not, somebody up here has an awful lot of loose bones.' Graveyard humour, she told herself. Why? It's only a fake, this wedding, but I'm feeling as if it was more than the real thing. Why?

'I don't know how you keep so cool,' Becky said. The little girl, dressed in a gown to match the bride's, although with a youthful Peter Pan collar and just barely reaching to her knees, was idly toying with the bridal bouquet. 'I'm scared to death!'

The little pump organ downstairs groaned a couple of times and began a fugue completely foreign to Marne's ear. Well, wasn't everything foreign? she asked herself. Mrs Willard, who played at the congregational church of a Sunday, had obliged. The organ itself was a real antique from the days when Pioneer Valley was really a frontier.

Mrs Willard played the organ at our first wedding. The church was packed and I hardly knew a soul. The organ was one of those huge multi-pipe instruments built into the rear wall of the chancel. I was terrified. When Gramps walked me into the vestibule I could feel the building shake from the power of that organ. Something old—one of Grandma's garters. Something new—a sparkling new wristband. Something borrowed? I can't remember now. Something blue—a tiny lace handkerchief, tucked into a fold of my gown. Lord, I was so terrified! And, as the marriage grew older, I don't think I ever stopped being terrified!

'Just one more thing,' Mrs Smith said. 'Rob sent you a bridal gift.'

The package was small; Marne's fingers fumbled with the wrapping over the little jewel box. When she opened the lid, sunlight sparkled. There was a concerted *ohhh*. 'But what is it?' Becky, too short to see, crowded her way to Marne's side.

'A jewel pin,' Marne said. 'Look. A sapphire fashioned in the centre of a little butterfly.' And I'm the only one who will understand the message, Marne told herself. How could so rotten a man be such a—wonderful fellow? A blue butterfly, the sign of faith, 'something blue'. Fidelity? I wish it were! A small tear began to trace itself under her eye. It's probably only a paste sapphire, she told herself grimly. A paste fidelity stone, for a fake wedding!

'None of that, now,' Mrs Smith chided. 'Do you want to wear it?' Marne nodded, to keep from crying.

'Up here, then, child, just under this little fold. Now, have we got it all? Something old, something new, something borrowed, something blue?'

'Everything,' Marne said, sighing. 'And a sixpence in my shoe. Isn't that the way the old rhyme goes?'

'Better take it out before the dancing starts,' practical Becky added.

'Then let's mount up,' her future and former mother-in-law commanded, 'and go down and scatter a few pearls.'

'I don't understand that, neither,' Becky complained.

'That's because you don't read your Bible often enough,' her grandmother commented. 'Here we go.'

They came down the stairs in a formal little parade. Mrs Smith first, serving as conductor. Becky next, her flood of blonde hair tucked up under a sweet circlet of field flowers, the shaking bride last, her head bent as she nibbled on her lower lip and prayed everything would go well. At the foot of the stairs Mrs Smith stepped aside, looking very self-satisfied indeed. A tall distinguished white-haired man stood by Mr Dixon and smiled. Marne combed her mind. Of course. Mr Burroughs. The man who had kept Peterboro in his political hip pocket, so to speak, for years. Mr Dixon proffered his arm to the bride, and Betsy Willard, at the organ, began to play.

Dixon could feel her shivering hand as she tried to restrain herself. He had known her all her life, both as student, confidant, and teacher in the Weldon Street Elementary School. 'Don't let it get to you,' he coaxed as the couple paused to let Becky get a head start. 'They're all friends. Keep your eye on that third row of chairs. If you decide to run for it, that's the place.'

Marne found her voice. 'I wouldn't dare,' she sighed, and the procession moved on. The big double parlour was full. In fact there were friends and youngsters out on the surrounding veranda, watching through all the open windows. The organ squeaked as one of the two boys doing the peddling missed his cue, and then it rose and drowned out the entire world. A couple of photographers were busy at their work. One of them, Marne vaguely noted, was a tall, beautiful raven-haired woman, whose name escaped her at the moment.

Marne sniffed up a couple of tears, and struggled to keep up the measured pace. *I will not cry!* Mr Dixon tightened his elbow as a sign of encouragement. The flower-drowned altar seemed to be a million miles away. The preacher, holding his Bible in one hand, was smiling. Rob was standing on the other side, smiling too. Why is it, Marne asked herself, that I just suddenly noticed—here, two steps away from marriage—what big teeth he has? Shark teeth? But before she could draw a conclusion her mind went off into a tail-spin. Mr Dixon drew her to a halt, kissed her on the cheek, and passed her hand over to Rob. And there, she told herself with a silent giggle, I've been given away. In this world of the 1990s, they're still giving girls away!

The organ wailed to a stop. Mr Hunter stepped forward. 'Dearly beloved,' he said, and those were the last words that Marne was to hear.

Somewhere in the middle of everything someone nudged her. 'I do,' she muttered. More words.

'With this ring—' and Rob was sliding a cold gold ring on her finger.

More words, and then, 'I now pronounce you man and wife.' All the sounds came to a halt. 'You may kiss the bride,' Mr Hunter prompted. Rob did. Gently, as if this fragile creature might break. It was the most chaste kiss Marne had received in the past five years. Congratulations thundered down on them from all sides. Marne Smith clung tightly to her husband's arm and prayed that she might not lose him in the crowd.

'And this is Mr Burroughs.' Rob made the introductions as they struggled though the crowd, heading for the door. 'Mr Burroughs has kindly agreed to show me the political ropes in this county.' A flashgun fired in their faces. The tall brunette behind the camera offered Marne a hungry-tiger smile. Rob seemed to have caught a frog in his throat. 'And his daughter Sylvia, who is also going to help out with publicity,' he managed to mumble. 'And now we'd better run.'

'You don't have time for a honeymoon,' Burroughs called. 'There's the American Legion caucus tomorrow night. You won't forget?'

'I won't forget,' Rob called. He tugged at Marne's arm and rushed her out of the door to where his station wagon was waiting. It was covered with ribbons, smothered with confetti, and surrounded by half a dozen boys, all of whom looked guilty of something.

'Don't forget me,' Becky wailed. Marne turned to look. The girl was still somehow carrying the bridal bouquet. Marne gestured; Becky tossed the flowers to her, and then backed off a step or two. At which time Marne threw the lucky piece back towards the crowd, but angled so that only Becky could catch it. There was a roar from the watchers. 'Fixed,' some woman in the back of the crowd yelled. And that was the last thing under Marne's control for the rest of that day.

'What's the hurry?' she yelled at Rob as he pushed her almost head first into the car and then struggled to start the engine.

'Custom,' he yelled back at her. 'We have to get out of the way so they can get on with the serious eating and drinking.' He shoved the car into gear, and off they went, with a trail of tin cans tied to the rear bumper, making sounds like the devil's chorus.

'Oh, lord,' Marne groaned.

'Not to worry,' her new husband said. 'Brains over brawn every time, love.' He drove the car for another hundred yards, down to the bend in the highway, and stopped. Waiting for them off the side of the road was a shiny Cadillac. 'Rented,' he observed as he swapped their luggage into the new car, crowded her into its regal silence, and then put his hands on her shoulders and turned her in his direction. 'All well done, Marne,' he said softly. 'Scared?'

'Petrified,' she reported. 'What do we do now?'

'Well, I told everyone we were going down to Springfield for the night.'

'But we won't?'

'But we won't. We're going to spend one night in the Tilson house. We need the rest. Tomorrow starts the rat race. I want to tell you how proud of you I was. Could you spare me a kiss?'

'Just one,' she half whispered. It was a respectable sort of kiss, the kind to start off her married life, Marne thought. But then something rattled in the back of her mind, demanding attention. This is a fake wedding, Marne Tilson. And this is the beginning of the first fake night. And you'd better get up on your toes, girl. Men's promises are perhaps not the most dependable things in the world.

So by the time she had that well chewed and settled in the front of her mind they were outside the Tilson house. He carried the luggage in and set it down in the kitchen. Marne came along slowly. 'I haven't done much today,' she said, 'but I'm tired. Terribly tired.'

'Just a darn minute,' Rob said. 'I have to carry you over the threshold.'

'There's nobody to watch,' Marne protested. 'You did that the first time, and it didn't work.'

'Maybe times will be better,' he said softly as he picked her up and carried her into the kitchen. 'I had a little something sent over by the caterer for supper here tonight. And in the meantime we ought to change out of all this finery, get cooled down, and relax. Where shall I put the bags?'

Marne's head snapped up. That tired I am not, she told herself. He had that disingenuous look in his eye again. 'That's easy,' she told him stiffly. 'Put *my* bags in *my* room, and yours in my mother's room. Was there ever any question?'

He shook his head. 'No, I guess not. But a man has to try, you know.' He was whistling as he packed the luggage away. Morgan, who had not been invited to the wedding feast, came out of the kitchen and took up watch. Marne walked tiredly into her own room and shut the door. Whistling, was he? That wouldn't last long.

The flowered coronet was beginning to bother her. She unpinned it, laid it down on top of her bureau. In the heat of the summer day the little buds were already fading. Some symbolism, she told herself. The wedding's over indeed! She gave her hair a good rub. The dress came off gently; even if the wedding was a fake, the dress was not. She knew that—for however long this wedding lasted—she would treasure the dress.

And what did a country bride wear after the wedding? *Nothing*?

That's what Rob had teased her with on their honeymoon night. She had been so nervous that she would not have been able to get out of the wedding gown had he not helped. And for some time he had kept her that way.

Marne's blushes ran rampant. She had been a virgin then. Now, to avoid further wild thoughts, she climbed into jeans and a blouse, and buttoned and zipped herself up completely.

He was waiting in the living-room as she came out. 'It's been a long day,' he murmured as he led her out on to the porch and on to the swing. 'Something bothering you?'

'Not exactly bothering,' she said. Her hair had all come down by now. She brushed it gently, then started it into a braid. 'I only wondered.'

'About what?'

'About your campaign—and Mr Burroughs.'

'Well, in the first place,' he replied, 'he really knows how to go about winning an election. He's had more experience than anyone in the county in raising election money. And that's the secret to success these days.'

'Yes,' she said, so softly that he barely heard. 'And my grandmother used to say that if you turned over every rock in the county you'd find either Burroughs or one of his men hiding—or maybe both.'

'Hey, don't pre-judge the man,' Rob said. 'He's done some fine things over the past few years. And he's always been nice to me.'

'I'll bet he has.' She made a little face at him, and he laughed.

'Well, if that's the hard question, we're in for a happy life.'

'For a happy campaign,' she amended. 'But that wasn't the hardest question I can think of.'

He looked down at her expectantly. She moved an inch or two away from him, and was grateful when Morgan jumped up into her lap. It gave her fingers something to do, scratching the old cat's ears.

'Tell me something.' He nodded. She stared out down the valley, afraid to let him see her eyes. They had always been her give-away eyes, unable to keep a secret from anybody. 'This Sylvia—the camera person. Isn't that the

woman that you——?' The words ran out. How did you ask
a man who invited his last inamorata to the wedding?

'That I met a few years ago? That's a fair question. The
answer is yes.'

'And you don't think we'll have trouble carrying off this
masquerade while she's hanging around?'

'I'm sure we won't,' he answered. She snapped her head
around to stare at him. He was nibbling at his lower lip.
The smile had gone.

'Sure we won't? Wouldn't it be safer not to have invited
her? I gather she means to work on the campaign?'

'That's your only fault,' he said, sighing. 'You're not
only too curious, but you're too bright. That's two questions. The answer to both is yes. She intends to work on
the campaign. Why I don't know. And we could have
avoided a great deal of trouble by not inviting her.'

'That's it? No explanation?'

'Damn you, Marne.' He pounded one of his big fists on
his knee. 'Don't you think the explanation is simple?'

She shook her head. Her long braid swung around her
head, and Morgan took a swipe at it. 'No,' she said, 'nothing's too simple for me.'

He jumped to his feet and started to pace back and forth.
The swing jumped and swayed, throwing Marne off-centre,
and out of her concentration. 'Let me draw you a picture,'
he snapped. 'Elections cost money. Lots of money. And
Burroughs knows where it's at. He wants his daughter to
help out. Period. End of discussion.'

'And Sylvia? I don't want to make any *faux pas* during
the campaign. Do you have a strong feeling for her?'

'Yeah, I have a very strong feeling,' he said bitterly. 'I'd
love to buy her a one-way ticket to Moscow. Come on,
let's eat something!'

'The master speaks,' Marne whispered to Morgan as she
got up and started for the kitchen. The cat ignored the

whole situation. Somebody had said 'eat', and that was one word that Morgan thoroughly understood.

Rob stopped her at the door, using a single finger on her shoulder to do so. 'What did you say?'

'Me?' Marne's mind raced at something more than the speed limit. 'I said the swing caster squeaks. I've been meaning to oil it for months.' She could almost feel his eyes boring into her back as she walked into the house. Mark that down, she told herself as she moved. The master has big teeth. The master also has big ears! Still, that wasn't so bad. He would never smack Sylvia in the mouth. Men like Rob Smith didn't do that sort of thing. But maybe I could help?

CHAPTER FOUR

'KEEP your teeth showing, no matter what happens,' Rob said as he escorted Marne up to the doors of the Milford Arms in Terryville, almost fifty miles from home.

'Don't lecture me as if I were some dumb kid,' she returned. 'I'm all grown up. That's one of the reasons I divorced you, Rob Smith. You needn't worry that I'll keep my teeth showing. Lord, I might want to bite half a dozen of them. And the food so far is awful.'

He pulled her to a stop. 'You mean that, Marne? About—before?'

'Of course I mean it. I know I was only a kid, but you treated me as if I were ten. Public or private. I felt like a wet rag most of the time. If I had had more courage I would have kicked—er—done you some violence—but, then, I didn't know very much about men back then. You scared me whenever you raised your voice.'

'I—never noticed,' he sighed. 'One more regret to carry around in my sack.'

'Well, we were both young, Rob. And now we're not. Come on, let's face the dragons. What is this, the fourth stop of the day?'

'Yes, but the third one didn't serve food.'

'That's a relief. I've been carrying bicarbonate lozenges in my bag for the last two weeks. Oh, good grief.'

'What now?'

'Look who's at the door, waiting for us.'

'It's only Sylvia, love, with the briefing papers. You know we couldn't survive the day without these little notes she makes up for me at every stop.'

'How could I forget?' Marne sighed. 'She does all your thinking for you. I get the funny feeling that it's a Burroughs campaign, not the Smith campaign. Just so long as she sticks to briefing papers, I suppose it's all right.'

'Don't get any ideas, Marne!' He tugged her a little closer and bent down to kiss her pretty nose. 'I do all of my own thinking. Well, most of it, anyway. I could almost believe you're jealous.'

It was dark, almost eight o'clock in the evening, and a light drizzle was setting in, for which Marne was grateful. At least he couldn't see her blush. It was four weeks since their second marriage. Marne's feet hurt, and so did her heart. It was becoming more and more difficult to keep from telling him the real truth—that her earlier love was fast returning.

'C'mon,' she said quickly, heading for the stairs.

'There's a small problem,' Sylvia announced as she handed Rob a set of small cards. 'There's no room at the head table for Marne. I've put her over at the side-table with the wife of one of the local officers.'

'Marne?'

'I don't mind,' she answered. 'Just so long as I get a chance to sit down.' She followed the pair of them into the hall. They were discussing the card-file information. Marne looked around. The hall was almost at capacity. Which, she knew, was a welcome sign. At seventy-five dollars a plate, this one meeting would considerably swell the campaign coffers. Her only trouble was she didn't know a soul outside of Rob's travelling team, and it bothered her. She wanted to help, but the campaign committee had shut the door firmly in her face. She was strictly a decoration. As now.

Rob came back to her, caught her in his arms, and kissed her, a real honeymoon kiss. And the crowd loved it. So did

Marne. 'How about another?' she asked as the applause rolled across the room.

'We don't have time,' Sylvia interrupted. 'We're on a tight schedule.'

'Aren't we always?' Rob said, disgusted. 'Well, there's your guide, Marne. I'll see you after the show.' And off he went, following Sylvia like a hound dog commanded to heel.

'My, he's such a handsome young man!'

Marne turned around to meet her own private welcoming committee. Two dowagers of a doubtful age, dressed in high fashion. So high that Marne furtively began to tug at her blue serge suit. It had been fourteen hours and almost a hundred miles since she had put it on back home. But a candidate's wife—she took a deep breath, and flashed her smile.

'Yes, he is,' she agreed. 'And he's all mine!' And wished it was true.

'It's good to be proud, but after we elect him sheriff you'll have to share,' her escort persisted. 'Ethel Norton, my dear. Vice-chairman of the town committee. We're so crowded that we've had to put our table over here in the back corner.'

'It doesn't matter.' Marne managed somehow to widen her smile. And besides, I've heard this speech three times today, she wanted to add, but didn't. Whether she wanted to or not, she was forced to admit that Rob was a brilliant speaker. No matter what he said, he left one with the distinct impression that things were going to shape up at the county jail if he was elected. She followed Ethel off into the corner, and sighed with relief as a white-haired gentleman held her chair for her. And it was only then that she noticed Sylvia sitting up on the dais next to her husband!

'I should have brought binoculars,' she said to Ethel,

seated next to her. 'We've not seen a crowd as big as this since the campaign started.'

'You should have been up at the head table,' her neighbour returned. 'I can't understand why your campaign manager said that we should change the seating plan.'

And neither do I, Marne thought. 'I really don't mind, Ethel.'

'Well, I do. Now I have to sit way back here in the corner, and I don't hear as well as I once did. Try the chicken.'

Marne looked down at her plate. 'I think I've seen this particular chicken before,' she murmured. Ethel evidently hadn't. She dug in, eating and talking at the same time.

'Any children, Mrs Smith? A sheriff ought to have a family.'

'Rather difficult. We've only been married for four weeks. But Rob has a little niece who has taken us under her wing. And yes, we plan to have a family of four, God willing.'

'That's nice.'

'Yes, Becky is very nice.'

'I meant the chicken is nice, my dear. It's so hard to get such a large gathering properly catered for.'

'Of course,' Marne returned as she attacked the chicken. Note number six: candidates' wives are meant to be seen and not heard. Once again she tugged at her blouse, trying to get it back in order. Candidates' wives. The phrase still had a strange sound. Candidates' wives. We'll be back home tonight, and I hope Morgan will be glad to see me.

Ethel put a hand on Marne's wrist, and pointed toward the dais. The speech-making had already begun, and Rob was introducing her. Obviously he didn't quite know where she had got to. Marne hastily scraped back her chair, stood up, and waved to the crowd. The spotlight operator obviously didn't know where she was either. The beam of his light wavered across the room twice before picking her out. And then Rob was off on his favourite subject, the laxity of discipline and care in the sheriff's department.

Marne sank back into her seat. 'That's nice,' Ethel said cheerfully. 'He has a wonderful speaking voice.'

'Amateur theatricals,' Marne returned. 'Years of amateur theatricals. He's a great actor.'

Chairs were scraping back all over the room as applause followed the speech. 'And you didn't even get to eat your chicken,' Ethel said mournfully.

'No problem,' Marne lied. 'I'm a vegetarian!'

The big limousine built up speed as they hit the highway. Marne did her best to curl up in the corner of the front seat. Rob had said not a word to her since the programme had ended. His eyes held the road as if driving was dangerous. Marne watched his arms as he drove. He had shucked his suit coat, and his short-sleeved shirt revealed the subtle play of a dozen muscles. She would have loved to cuddle up against him as she always had during their first marriage. But he looked too forbidding.

'It was a good crowd,' she offered. Silence. 'Ethel says you're bound to get elected. A sure thing.'

'Ethel. Who the hell is Ethel?'

Marne giggled. 'Mrs Ethel Norton is the vice-chairman of the town committee. Only I don't remember what town we're in.'

'Terryville,' he muttered. 'Why the hell did you go off and hide away in that back corner?'

Marne stiffened. 'I didn't just *go off*,' she stated firmly. 'I was directed. Ethel tells me that your campaign manager asked for the change. There wasn't enough room on the dais, she said.' But there was plenty of room for Sylvia Burroughs! But why should I be so damn jealous? It isn't as if this were the real thing, this marriage of ours.

'My campaign manager? Burroughs?'

'How should I know? How many managers do you have?'

'And what's that supposed to mean?'

'I don't know, do I? I'm just the little country girl that married you. What is it, Rob? Is Mr Burroughs doing all the planning *and* thinking for you? Every once in a while I have to look closely to make sure your puppet-strings aren't showing.'

The tyres on the big car squealed as he applied the brakes and drove them off on to the hard shoulder. 'Now that's a hell of a thing to say, Marne. I do my own thinking. What's eating you?'

'Eating me? Nothing's eating me.'

'That's not what Sylvia says.'

'Oh? And now you're listening to the girl who's been campaigning like mad. You know it's you she wants, Rob, not the sheriff's office.'

There was nothing urbane about this man next to her, not now. His voice had become rough as he reached across the seat and grabbed her by the shoulders. 'Well, at least she—'

'She what? Go ahead and say it.'

'She has the courtesy to defer to my judgements, rather than criticise me out of the corner of her mouth,' he snapped.

'And that's what I did? Is that the charge, Sheriff? Are you going to put the cuffs on me and take me in? I take it you have a secret informer?'

'Yes,' he groused. 'Sylvia keeps me posted.'

'And she could hear everything I had to say, with her on the dais and me in the back corner?'

'Damn it, Marne, there's nothing going right in all this.'

'Oh? I thought the campaign was going ahead great guns.

There's only another two weeks before the primary election, isn't there?'

'I don't mean the campaign. To hell with the campaign. I mean between you and me!'

Marne's heart skipped a beat. Between you and me? Was there ever again to be something 'between you and me'? I want desperately to have something to go on between us, she told herself. But—but everything that goes around comes around. And here you are, playing games again with Sylvia Burroughs.

'I—don't think there is anything that ought to be going on between you and me,' she stated primly. 'After all, I'm only doing you a favour, marrying you again. Don't you remember? A fake marriage?'

'Marne—' He seemed to have got his tongue trapped between his teeth. 'You haven't ever thought to make it all real?'

'Our marriage? Not recently,' she said. 'Not since Sylvia popped up in the middle of things.' She coiled herself up on the seat again. 'I really don't want to talk about this, Rob. I really don't.'

He made a noise. Under the soft rumble of the engine, the clacking of the windscreen wipers, the patter of the rain, he made a noise. Or said something? Marne didn't dare to ask. It was almost like a groan. But that could hardly be, could it?

And then he shifted the car back into gear, and took off down the highway for home.

'Better be careful,' she challenged him bleakly. 'You wouldn't want the sheriff's patrol to give you a ticket, would you?'

She heard what he said next. It was an unrepeatable word. The last word he had to say until they pulled up in front of the house.

Rob set the handbrake and shut down the engine with a

flourish. 'There. We now have a whole weekend to ourselves.'

'Good.' Marne stretched and opened the door. 'Sleep. That's what I want. Why in the name of all that's holy do we have to run around the county like a cat with its tail cut off?'

'That's the way elections are run,' he said gruffly. 'See the voter eyeball to eyeball. Press the hands. Pontificate. There are thirty-six towns and villages and cities in this county. And before the election I want to be seen in every one of them—'

'You'll make it,' she interrupted. 'Kiss the babies. Now there's a nice thought.'

'What? Kissing babies?'

'No, just babies. I like babies. Did we make enough money this time so you can buy a little radio advertising time?'

'I don't know,' he said. 'Burroughs looks after all of that side of things.'

'Burroughs, Burroughs, Burroughs,' she mocked. 'I wonder why *he* isn't running for sheriff?'

'He can't. He's running for the state senate. Come on, woman. We're here. Let's get inside before we drown.' Before she could escape he put his suit jacket around her shoulders. The instant comfort was there. Not because the night was cool, which it was, but because it was *his* coat. It smelled and breathed and lived of him. She could hear the little pulse in her ear crying Rob, Rob, Rob!

Marne stumbled up the steps in front of him, dodging the point where the gutter leaked and sprayed cold water on unwary necks. He brushed by her and fumbled with the key. The interior of the house was cold. Even in the late summer the mountain chill had set in.

'Morgan's not here.' When you had lived with a particular cat for a large part of your life, missing was noticeable.

He came in close behind her, lifting the wet coat from her shoulders immediately. 'Probably Becky kept her at the other house. Morgan never was a rain-lover, was she?'

Marne collapsed into the rocking-chair. Rob turned on one of the lamps, dropped his case, and did the same. 'Sometimes I wonder if it's worth it,' he said, sighing. 'Feet hurt?'

'You know they do,' Marne said. This *is* a throwback, she told herself as he sat down on the floor in front of her, removed her shoes, and began a gentle massage of the bottoms of her feet. Something he had done so often years ago. Something—loving.

Under the ministrations she began to let go. Her eyes grew heavy. She shifted her weight in the chair to rest one hip. His fingers moved across the bottoms of her feet. Did Cleopatra have a slave who gave foot-rubs? she asked herself just before she went to sleep.

Rob continued the massage for a moment or two after he heard that tiny whistle of breath that she always emitted just when she went to sleep. God, I'm tired, he told himself as he finally pulled himself up on to his own feet. And *is* it worth it? he asked. No, not the political office. If she ever knew what a frame-up *that* was. But how else could I get this near to her? He rubbed his hand through his thick hair, and stretched. Kissing babies? How in the world did *that* ever come up?

It had been an intermittent argument between them for the whole of their first marriage. 'You've got the law and outside interests,' she would complain. 'I want a baby.' But how could you explain to a woman of eighteen that she was too much of a baby herself? Or that a struggling law student couldn't afford the extra expense? Or the real truth—I want you to myself for a little while yet? So no baby. One more stack of fuel to put on top of our bonfire.

'But I wish,' he said softly, almost under his breath, 'I wish I really knew what put the flame to the fire!'

Marne's rocking-chair squeaked. Time to move her into her bed. Into *our* bed, he thought as he walked across to her bedroom, opened up the bed, and turned on the night-light. Another little fetish. She always needed a night-light. Not because she was afraid of the dark. She wasn't really afraid of anything. Except me?

He came back and picked her up with all the gentleness of which he was capable. She stirred, shifted her weight in his arms, and cuddled up against his chest almost as if she were purring. He could feel the warmth of her breasts press-ing against him. It's worth the risk, he told himself. He kissed her again, once on the forehead, and once on that little nose.

She giggled when he put her down on the bed. Giggled, and then rolled over on to her side and pulled her knees up against her chest. It made a problem which he was happy to attack. Her blouse came off with no difficulty. His fingers plucked at the buttons cautiously, and seemed to touch on the softness of her breast by accident. Accident, he told himself as he went back for another taste of heaven. Yeah, accident! Not until she stirred uneasily did he give it up.

For the rest, he was out of practice, but he managed to strip her down before he tucked her into the long silk night-gown. One blanket was sufficient. He pulled it up to her chin. She was smiling. For a moment Rob Smith stood beside the bed and watched his wife sleep—and wished he had the nerve to crawl in beside her and make a real mar-riage out of all this.

Marne woke up with a smile. Morgan was lying across her stomach, making cat-sounds. The sun was bright in the sky. Saturday morning. A free day. There must be an easier way to elect a sheriff than all this, she told herself as she slipped

out of bed and fumbled into her slippers. The cat opened
one eye. 'Becky's come and gone?' Marne asked. The cat
gave her a wise nod, and began licking at her front paws.
'So don't talk,' Marne said, and stood up.

Somebody in the front of the house was talking. Some
man. Marne's smile widened. Something nice had happened to her in the night-time. She couldn't remember quite
what it was, but it involved Rob and herself. Maybe it was
only a dream? She took a step or two towards the bedroom
door, and then remembered how transparent her silk night-
gown was. But not how she came to be wearing it.
Speculation could be a nice thing. She shrugged her shoulders and reached for her robe.

It wasn't Rob talking, out there in the kitchen. In fact it
was three perfect strangers. Three rather large men, all of
whom came to their feet as she came in.

'Do I know why you're drinking coffee in my kitchen?'

'No. I suspect not.' The speaker was the elder of the
three, equipped with a fringe of white hair and a solemn
expression. 'Dirk Wilson, Mrs Smith. We are—er—a part
of your husband's campaign committee.'

She waved them back into their chairs. 'Oh, are you really? Strange that I've never seen you in these parts before.'

'Well—we're a part of the advance team,' Wilson said.
'May I make you known to Mr Jones and Mr Smith?' He
waved a hand vaguely in the direction of his compatriots.

Marne laughed, her full-throated weekend laugh. 'That's
my line, Mr—Wilson, is it? I'm the Smith around here.
People call me Marne. Or is this gentleman Smyth with a
"y"?'

'I—er—your husband—'

'My husband what? Absconded with the campaign treasury?' There was an instant silence in the room. All three
of them looked as if she had just released one of the secrets
of the space rocket!

'I said something wrong? Where *is* my husband?'

'He went into town,' Wilson said. 'There are one or two people he had to talk to, so he suggested we could do our work here. He also said he would bring back a pint of coffee ice-cream.'

Marne sat back in her chair, her eyes sparkling devilment. 'You see,' she commented. 'He's a devil, that man, but he sweeps me off my feet with coffee ice-cream. Just what work is it that you three do?'

'Surveys,' Mr Jones said firmly. 'Surveys.'

'Let me pour you a cup of coffee,' Wilson offered. All of them looked nervous. And then a car horn sounded outside, and they looked agitated.

'It's that Burroughs woman,' Jones said from his position behind the dimity kitchen curtain.

'My God,' one of the others commented. 'How bad can things get? Mrs Smith, do you suppose you could point out some place where the three of us might—work? We would hate to be seen by Miss Burroughs.'

'Me too,' Marne chuckled. 'Well, look, if it's all that serious, you could all three of you duck into the front parlour. Through there.' She watched as they hustled out. 'And be careful,' she called after them. 'My grandmother had that room stuffed to the roof with bric-a-brac.'

So they didn't care to be seen by Sylvia? Marne circled the table, picked up the used coffee-cups, and dumped them in the sink. She was in fine fettle. She loved mysteries—especially murder mysteries. And this scene had suddenly become a part of a best-seller plot. Just in time, for the raven-haired woman knocked once on the screen door and burst into the house as if it were hers by divine right.

'Well—Marne Smith.'

'I believe so. Isn't that what it says on the mailbox?'

'Always clever, Marne.' Sylvia wrinkled her nose, as if

something smelled bad. 'Too bad you're not clever enough.'

'But I'm a "wannabe",' Marne said. 'I'm just as clever as I wannabe. What brings you to the Smith house? Rob isn't here.'

'I know that, silly. He's downtown, meeting with my father. He asked me to come out and pick up some papers for him. He left them in his briefcase.'

'Briefcase? Of course, it's on top of *our* bed.' A major lie that seemed to startle Burroughs. 'I'll get it for you.' Marne got up and nipped over into Rob's room. Luckily the door to *her* bedroom was closed. The briefcase was on the chair beside his bed. She swept it up and brought it out.

'Anything else? A cup of coffee?'

'No, I—well, maybe I should. We haven't talked in such a long time.'

Marne provided the service, and topped off her own mug. 'No, we haven't talked, have we, Sylvia? What would you like to talk about?'

'Oh, I don't know. How about, what happens after the election?'

'Sounds fine. You start.'

Sylvia managed a little trill of laughter that ran upscale for a full octave. 'Well, of course, after the election you won't be needed, Marne. Have you ever thought of moving to Connecticut? I hear there are plenty of teaching jobs down there—at a good pay too. I'm sure my father would be glad to give you a recommendation.'

Look at the nerve of that woman, Marne thought. Wait until after the election and then move in? 'Is this something you've planned out with Rob?'

'Of course. After the election Rob is going to join my father's little group. You know, we'll have full control of all western Massachusetts then.' The brunette offered a glacial smile as she sipped her coffee. 'But by that time Rob will need a more…elegant helpmate. Let's face it, Marne. You didn't have it all those years ago, and you don't have it now. I'm sorry that you've been sleeping with Rob. That will all have to go, you know. You wouldn't want to tie him down now, would you?'

'I don't know about that,' Marne drawled. 'You know—no, you wouldn't know. Rob is a great performer under the sheets. I might well want to tie him down. Hog-tie him, that is.'

The beauty across the table became incensed. Her ivory face flushed as she pushed back her chair. It crashed to the floor. 'Damn you, Marne Smith,' she snarled. 'There's no use you struggling. You're a dead issue. I—my dad and I—have Rob already tied up in knots. He's on our team, and when we take on a new player we take him lock, stock and barrel!'

'Third strike?' Marne mounted a smile large enough for the occasion. 'You've had two times at bat already, Sylvia, and you haven't scored. What makes you think that you can make it this time?'

The brunette dropped her mug. It crashed on the table and rolled to the floor. Sylvia was so angry that she couldn't speak. Marne pushed on.

'You know, Sylvia, I meant to ask you, did you send me a videotape some years ago?'

'I—' Whatever it was Sylvia was about to say went by the boards. There came a loud sneeze from the front parlour. 'What's that?'

'That?' Marne improvised. 'That was my cat, Morgan. When she sneezes it sounds like a fire horn. Why don't you go away, Sylvia?'

'I'll go when I'm ready!'

'You could get a heart attack that way,' Marne said. 'You're ready, lady.' And while Sylvia gabbled, Marne seized her upper arm and walked her out of the house and over to her car. 'And do me a favour, Miss Burroughs. It's hard enough for me to get along with you on campaign days; don't risk your life by coming around my home again. Got it?'

The fancy sports car spun its wheels and sped away. Morgan tramped out and sat down beside Marne. 'She didn't get it,' Marne said. Her cat waved her abbreviated tail in agreement. Mr Wilson stuck his head out though the kitchen door.

'Is the coast clear?'

'The coast is clear,' Marne said, chuckling. 'You know, I've always meant to dust that parlour, but it's been two years and I haven't gotten around to it yet.'

CHAPTER FIVE

'IT'S SEPTEMBER and that's the end of the campaign?' Marne groaned as she fitted herself into the front seat of the car. 'I've been to two breakfasts, three lunches, and two teas just today!'

'Brave girl,' Rob said as he wheeled the car out on to Main Street. 'There will be three or four promotions by radio tonight, and one TV spot on the Springfield television station, and that's it. As far as you and I are concerned, all we have to do is sit back and wait for the polls to open tomorrow morning.' One of his big hands came off the wheel and patted her knee gently. 'Good show, love.'

'Ah!' She felt like doing something silly, like barking at him, for example. Or licking his paw? Love? Instead she shifted over in the seat to be close against him, pulled her legs up on to the seat, and laid her head down on his shoulder. He blew the horn and waved at a couple of prospective voters hurrying through the cool sunshine. She wrapped both hands around his arm and held on for dear life. It felt good. Almost as good as once it had been, years ago.

At the corner of Bilt Street he paused. 'Will you look at that?' he said.

'Look at what?'

He pointed across the street, where heavy construction equipment was busy. 'They're tearing down the Odeon Theatre, that's what.'

'The old movie theatre?'

'That's the place the Peterboro Players used to rent. Back when we thought we were bound to be a success. Don't you remember?'

163

'Not really,' she replied. 'I remember you being gone night after night, but I never actually tied it in to the theatre. Well, I guess all the old houses are falling, aren't they?'

'Yes,' he said. 'But this one had memories. We *all* thought we'd be starring on Broadway some day.'

'And now you're going to be sheriff.' She did her best to soothe, but he didn't need it.

He laughed as he turned to her. 'Sheriffing is steady employment, love. There are lots of actors on the breadline these days.' He offered the old building a tip of his cap, and drove on down Main Street.

Tired, but not exhausted, Marne dropped into a daydream as he followed the well-worn path out Main Street, up the hill on Darcey, and then out on to the old Albany Turnpike. Things were what they had been so long ago. When I didn't know any better, she told herself. And that brought a glum little chill.

'Asleep?'

'No. Just sort of dreaming. Will your goons be at the house this afternoon?'

'My goons?'

'You know. Jones and Smith and that other guy, who've been camping out with us for the past four days?'

'Oh, them. No. They've finished up all their work. We may have to do one more round tonight, but it's nothing you would want to participate in, so you don't have to worry.'

'That sounds pretty ominous.' She moved her head just far enough so she could study his rigid jawline, his cat-like eyes—and the little furrow in his forehead that made him look so young. 'I thought maybe we might just...rest this afternoon. Becky and your mother have the cat, and if your goons are gone we could—' She stopped in midstream. What she wanted to do was not on the bill. But nervous little spasms were running up and down her spine, and she—well, she wanted to. Unless he felt that they—God, how did I ever get in such a mess?

'Yeah,' he said as the heavy car began to climb the hill. 'A little rest, a light lunch—'

'Don't say food to me for the next thirty days,' Marne interrupted. 'Why is it that so many women wanted to gawk at me? Is there some magic to being the sheriff's wife?'

'An American custom, love. They want to believe that they're electing a perfectly normal, honest fellow, with a perfectly normal, honest wife, who aren't going to go charging off into some wild misadventure. They want to touch and see and hear—and maybe even smell, for all I know. Here we are.'

Marne unwound and climbed out without waiting for him. Her grey suit—the second of her two campaign suits—was as wrinkled as she felt. 'I need a shower,' she called back to him as she disappeared into her bedroom to pick up the necessaries, and then walked over into the bath-room.

'Me too,' Rob called after her. 'Don't use up all the hot water.'

Lucky he reminded me, Marne thought. Now *that* was something he had always yelled at her about, using up all the shower water and leaving him nothing. Giggling to her-self, she slipped out of her clothes and dumped them all into the hamper.

There was plenty of water. She ducked into its warm embrace and soaped to her heart's content. We used to do it together, she thought. Especially on Saturday afternoon. That was—why can't we do it again? We're married. We have a licence from the Commonwealth, and the blessings of the church. Why did I ever get myself into this unholy mess? I should have gone into a convent. Methodists don't have convents. What am I blustering about. Excited, she gently massaged her breasts with the soapy washcloth. Her reactions increased.

She turned off the water and climbed out. Steam covered the wall mirrors and condensed on the wash basin. The bath towels were large and well-worn. One more thing she had let go to the dogs during the past few years. She wrapped herself up cosily in one of them, and scrubbed herself dry. Leave one towel for Rob, she admonished herself. And where did I leave my robe? Not in the bedroom? A quick search of the bathroom. Yes, in the bedroom.

A small smile touched her lips. The devil made easy the paths to hell. How often she had heard that sermon! I can't walk across the house naked to get my robe, can I? The smile became a grin. Carefully she fashioned her towel into a sarong and tucked it in just over her breasts, and patted herself down. Yes, she thought, there's more of me than there used to be. I wonder if he really *would*— A knock thundered on the door.

'Come on, chum, don't take all day.'

Marne skidded over to the door and partially opened it. The warm air of the bathroom ran into the cooler air of the kitchen, and a fine fog formed. 'I didn't know there was a timer running,' she told him saucily. He was leaned against the doorjamb, balanced on one hand, with a towel fastened loosely around his waist. It was the first time she had seen so *much* of him in many a year. Her pulse began to race; surely he must see?

'I—' She fumbled for a word or two as she tried to sidle past him. Her foot came down on the cool linoleum of the kitchen, and she slipped.

Marne yelped.

'Don't worry, I've got you.' He seemed to be hardly straining as he snatched her up. 'Wouldn't do to have my wife fall—' Something snapped between them. Some electrical something that startled them both. He had snatched her up, but had missed her towel. It fluttered momentarily and then fell to the floor, catching at *his* towel as it went. As God had intended with Adam and Eve, they stood within each other's grip, stark naked.

'Oh, God.' Marne sighed as her hands went up around his neck and held on for dear life. Rob said not a word, but cuddled her close against him, moving her gently back and forth so that her nipples rubbed against his chest.

'Yes.' He was breathing heavily, as if he had just run the marathon. She wiggled against him, noting how quickly he had been aroused.

'Yes,' she whispered. It had been so long, but memory was quickly refreshed, in all its wild panoply of excitement.

'Yes,' he muttered, and carried her across the room and into her bedroom. The bed had been made up early in the morning, before they had hit the campaign trail. Somehow he managed to hold her with one arm, and used the other to strip back the blankets. She was trembling; so much so that when he gently stretched her out on the cold sheets another shiver hardly mattered.

'Don't,' she muttered.

'Don't?'

'Don't just stand there, looking,' she said.

'Oh.' The bed shook as his weight came down next to her. Instant warmth prevailed. His arm came up over her, and his fingers toyed with the lobe of her ear. 'Damn!'

'What?'

'Earrings,' he complained. 'How can I nibble an ear when you're wearing—'

'I'm a big girl,' she interrupted. 'There are plenty of other places to nibble.'

Whatever answer he made was lost as he found a spot for nibbling—the rose tip of her breast. Waves of tension swept over Marne, culminating in a rising climax as his soft tongue teased her most vulnerable spot. Nerves she had forgotten came into play as her breast hardened. His hand moved and landed on her other breast. He teased a nipple between his thumb and forefinger, all the while continuing to cherish the other.

Marne squirmed a little lower in the bed. His tongue followed. Her excited little hand swept up over the rise of his belly, toyed with his navel, ran up and down his chest. He groaned, and shifted his attention to her mouth. His tongue pursued hers; she opened her lips to welcome the invasion, moaning all the while.

Another change. His hand shifted down the hill of her breast, and gently coursed farther, until it reached her ultimate precipice and plunged over. In the darkness where her most sensitive part hid, his fingers found their goal. It was hard to suppress the little squeak as he discovered the right place, and began that most refined of all tortures.

Marne squirmed in the sheer delight of it all, wiggling slightly from side to side, and then upward, as if she wanted to escape his terrorism, but of course it wasn't true. She did not want to escape, only to gain a few inches of space so that she could plunge down hard on him. He laughed at the contact.

'Do it,' she muttered. She was bathed with perspiration, panting for breath, seared by fire. 'Do it,' she whispered.

Not too reluctantly Rob rolled over on top of her, took a moment to kiss the tip of her nose, and then slid down into position between her legs. 'Do it,' she urged hoarsely. He did it.

Time had a peculiar function. In moments like this, time slowed almost to a crawl as he plunged into her, as deeply as flesh would allow. And then time sped as he pumped in and out. Marne, riding the wild beast almost to an end, did her best to regulate her thrusts to his, with no luck. His hands shifted from her shoulders to under her buttocks, where his superior strength took her into his own rhythm.

For another frantic moment they beat against each other until finally, with a massive groan, he thrust even deeper, and locked himself into her while his juices flowed and mingled and brought her to an excruciating peak. For just a moment they lay there rigid, two made into one, and then he collapsed on top of her, utterly spent.

His weight was an apostrophe to the exercise. He stirred once as if to withdraw. Her small hands wrapped themselves around him and held him. 'Don't move,' she said, sighing. His head rested just over her shoulder, perspiration dripping from his forehead. She wiped it away with a casual hand.

'Oh, my,' he offered. Marne laughed with the joy of it.

'"Oh, my," is that all you have to say?'

'Yes.'

'You used to be more vocal.'

'I was younger then. Did I hurt you?'

'No, not in the slightest. It's been a long, long time. You never—'

'No, I never did. Not ever with anyone else, Marne. I didn't have the spirit for it. But you've certainly improved.'

'I spent a thousand nights, Rob, rehearsing how it had been, what I had done wrong. How I could have made it better.'

'You've certainly learned from experience.'

'No, I can't say that I did. Just at that moment—out by the bathroom door, I completely forgot everything that I'd studied!' A moment of silence as he unfettered her, and lay by her side.

'Rob?'

'I think I bit you too hard in all the excitement.'

'It is a little sore, but it'll get better. I've got two of them. Rob?'

'What?'

'When we were first married you always said a good man could do it twice without any trouble.'

'Which just goes to show you what a bloody fool I was. I could do it two or three times in those days, but not anywhere near as well as we did just then. I love you, Marne.'

'I'm glad.'

'What are you doing now?'

'Well, I thought if I encouraged it a little bit, we—'

'You're on the right track, glutton.'

'Glutton? Well, if you'd rather not do it again, all you have to do is say so.' She spoke primly, and patently falsely.

'If I want you to stop I'll tell you,' said the superior male. 'Oh, lord, now what?'

There came a knock on their front door. A thundering, smashing knock. And a voice calling. 'Marne? Granny asked me to bring Morgan back. She's nervous or something, so I—'

'Becky! No! Don't come in. We're—'

'*Your* niece. I don't know when I'd have been less glad to see her.'

'Where the devil are my trousers?'

'In your room, I suspect.' Marne, a broad grin on her face, lay back against the pillows and admired his firm male body as he frantically searched for something to cover himself.

'What are you smirking at?' he growled as he paused in the search. 'You're as badly off as I am.'

'Me? Why, Mr Smith! I'm in *my* bedroom in *my* bed, covered by *my* blanket. How can you accuse me of anything?' Her delightfully contralto laugh followed him as he abandoned his search and made a dash for his own room.

Of all the things Becky Smith, the ten-year-old busy-body, would never think to do, one was to wait to be invited. As in this case. After one more carolling announcement Becky burst into the house and came directly to Marne's bedroom.

'I brung your cat,' she said as she walked through the door and dropped Morgan on the bed. 'She was sick for somethin'. I think she misses you. What are you doing in bed at four o'clock in the afternoon? Are you sick, Marne? Do you want I should call the doctor?'

The lovely green eyes grew wider as her uncle came in behind her. Rob had managed to find an old brown robe, and had slipped into it. His hair was wet. Evidently he had detoured by the bathroom. The little girl's eyes grew wider.

'What the devil are you doing here at four in the afternoon?' her uncle lectured her. 'Can't we have any privacy at all?'

'Don't be so mean,' Marne cautioned. 'She just came to see about Morgan. Becky?' But the little girl stared as her eyes grew wider, and then she covered her mouth with both hands and ran for the door.

Her uncle started after her. 'So you brought the cat back. Now scoot.'

'I gotta tell Granny,' the child said.

'Don't you dare,' Rob yelled after her, but the child was out of the door before he could think of anything positive to do.

'Don't waste your time,' Marne told him as she sat up in the bed. His eyes shifted. She looked down to where he was focused, and pulled the blanket up. 'She'll be halfway home before you could get your trousers on!'

'But... Do you think she knows?' he stammered.

'Of course she knows. Modern education,' Marne told him. 'They teach all that stuff in the schools, Mr Smith. You should be proud that our school system does so well!'

'Well, I'd damn well prefer that they teach her reading and writing,' he muttered, 'and leave sex alone!'

'Old-fashioned,' Marne chuckled. 'The schools have so many subjects to teach that reading and writing hardly qualify any more.'

'That girl has a tongue that's hinged in the middle,' he grumbled. 'By tomorrow this little tale will be over half the county.'

'Fearful for *your* reputation?' Marne asked. 'Lord, how times have changed. I would have thought you'd be concerned about *my* reputation.'

His face looked as if he had just run into a block of cement. 'See here, Marne—' he started to say, and then the telephone rang. 'I'll get it. We have to talk, woman.'

Marne watched him go, like a Roman centurion in a hurry, with an invisible sword strapped at his side. So? We have things to talk about, do we? Well, let me tell you, Rob Smith, just make sure there's no more subterfuge going on around here. No more lies. No more video scenes with Sylvia Burroughs in the middle of them. Let's make sure, shall we? No more of that massive male domination. Partnership. Share and share alike. If you can do that, Mr Smith, we might have an excellent—superior—relationship.

Through the open door she could hear her husband at work with the telephone. 'Blown wide open, you say?' A pause for the other side of the conversation. 'They know everything now?' Another pause. 'Damn that woman. I'd like to hang her from a sour apple tree.'

Sylvia Burroughs, Marne told herself. Who else could qualify in the whole of this county? Let it be Sylvia. I *want* it to be Sylvia. If we had a guillotine I'd volunteer to pull the cord! Are you listening, lord?

'Well, there's no use crying about it,' Rob said to whomever he had on the line. 'All right. That's a go on everything. Pass the word. Everything goes immediately!' The telephone slammed back into its cradle, and in a moment Rob walked back into her bedroom.

By this time Marne had recovered her aplomb, and allowed her blanket to slip a few inches south of the crests of her breasts. But he wasn't looking this time. 'Now, shall we take up where we left off?' she proposed in the most sultry voice she could muster.

'I—we'll have to put it off for a while,' he said. She could hear the strain in his voice, the worry. 'There just isn't time,' he continued. 'I've got a fire-storm running through the middle of my business.'

'Running for sheriff requires a fire-storm?'

'No—I—you wouldn't understand, Marne. I have to go.'

'Explain to me first,' she insisted. 'I'm twenty-six years old, with a college degree and a very large curiosity bump. Election day isn't until tomorrow. I'm working on a fire-storm of my own, Mr Smith. You couldn't postpone this trouble of yours for—say—another hour or so?'

'No, I can't,' he mumbled. 'I've got to go. I have no idea what time I might get back. Why don't you—er—take a little nap or something? Curl up with a good book?'

'Yes, I'll do that,' Marne said coolly. 'A good book, that ought to take your place well enough.' He had gone next door, and made noises like a big man dressing in a hurry. When he came back in he was fully prepared to go.

'Yes,' he said anxiously. 'Find a good book. I'll be back as soon as I can. We've got a million things to talk about.'

'Yes, we have,' she said softly. 'This had better all be true, Rob. If I find another deception afloat in all this mess you can expect the fastest divorce in the county. Fool me once, shame on you. Fool me twice, shame on me.'

'There's nothing like that,' he maintained, but he had to wipe his brow, and she noticed the tell-tale jitter at his fingers.

'No, of course not,' she agreed, but there was the taste of disbelief behind the words. 'Run along, Rob. I'll be here when you get back.'

'Marne?'

'What?'

'We'll make it a real marriage. Children and all?'

'We'll see. You'd better hurry. The voters must be champing at the bit.'

'Voters? Oh—yes, the voters. Keep warm, love.' He leaned over and kissed her gently. In no way was it like his kisses of the past hour or so; still, it was a sincere and promising thing. The sort of kiss a married lady could well be glad to receive.

'Be careful,' he added, and was gone.

Marne Smith stretched out on her bed, and flexed her stiffening arms over her head. What a marvellous day this has been, she thought. Not since God invented nice days— have I had such a nice day. She squeaked in delight as she settled back to recall it all. Rapid eye movement set in before she could sum up the first scene. She turned over on her side, with a huge smile on her face, her legs drawn up into her chest. In a moment that thin little whistle could be heard. Morgan, eager for something more sustaining than conversation, heard the whistle and knew her luck had run out. Marne slept the sleep of the faithful.

CHAPTER SIX

ROB was gone for the longest time. Marne slept, awoke, made herself a scrambled-egg sandwich, and slept again. And still he didn't come. There was nothing on television. The local radio stations were busy with their pop tunes. After the fervour of the primary campaign it almost seemed as if someone had turned off the whole world.

Of course, it wasn't entirely true. Her *Morning Herald* came at seven the next morning, as usual. But it had been put to bed early the night before, and contained practically nothing—except a fervent plea for everyone to get out and vote.

Panic-stricken, Marne telephoned her mother-in-law. 'No, we haven't heard a word,' Mabel Smith reported. 'There were a couple of his men staying here, but they rushed off yesterday afternoon, and I haven't heard boo from them since. Would you like to come over and stay with me, Marne?'

'I th-think…' she stammered. I think I'd better get to bed and hide my head under the blankets. I think—lord, I don't know what I think.

'I think I'd better run down and vote. And then better come back here. But—he's missing. Do you think I'd better call the police? No? Well, then, I'd better get downtown and back. There's no telling when he might come back— or call. Oops, there's someone ringing my front doorbell. I'll bet it's him. G'bye, love.'

So excited was she that she missed the telephone cradle, and had to pick the instrument up off the floor. Marne dashed for the front door and threw it open.

'Rob, where—?' But it was not Rob. Two men stood on her doorstep. Two men she did not know. One carried a large camera.

'Isaac Stone,' the first man introduced himself. 'And my cameraman. We're from the *Herald*. Is it true that your husband—?' Marne waved them through, and led them to the living-room, where the reporter had a great deal to say, and left her, dazed, after a half a hundred refusals on her part to answer his questions.

'Thank God that's over,' Rob Smith said to his three companions as they pulled up in front of the house. 'Now, I intend to be hard to find. You people follow up all the charges, and don't call me unless the British threaten to burn Washington.'

'What?'

'That's a joke, George. Don't call me at all. Right?'

'Say, Rob.' A comment from the back seat, where his two accountants sat. 'I think you've got some trouble here.'

'Trouble here?' Rob looked up at the porch. Two suitcases and a raincoat sat at the top edge of the stairs. 'Oh, my God.'

'Yours or hers, Rob?'

'Shut up and get out of here, you guys. Move.'

There was a little plume of dust as the back wheels of the car sought traction in the dirt of the parking space. Rob climbed the stairs. It was close on seven o'clock in the evening of election day. And the suitcases were his own.

'Marne?' Morgan sounded off a greeting as he opened the screen door. 'Marne?' He heard the dry sob from the living-room. His legs seemed suddenly to be heavy. His mind raced. There *had* to be a solution to the problem, but what? It required no genius to know that Marne Smith had found out about his little game.

'The finest bust in the last ten years,' the district attorney had told him not more than an hour ago. But how to explain that to the girl who sat dry-eyed in the rocking-chair in front of the television set? Dry-eyed, and yet crying.

'I'm back, Marne.' She looked up at him, her face contorted, and then back at the television set.

'Marne?'

'I see. I packed your bags for you. There's no need to stay, now that the election is over.'

'Marne, I don't *want* to leave. I intend to stay, come hell or high water.' He walked over to her chair and knelt in front of her. Her foot, which had been rocking the chair, stopped. The woman acted as if she were frozen into stone. And the only thing that will melt it all is love, he told himself.

She made no resistance as he pulled her forward into his arms. No resistance, and no reaction. It was like hugging a rag doll.

'It's not going to be like last time,' he said firmly. 'I had no chance for a hearing then. This time you're going to listen.'

It must have been something in his tone of voice that activated her. She looked down at him, and a tear formed in her eye. 'There's no need to tell me anything,' she said in a whisper. 'They have it all over the tube.'

'There are things that the TV people don't know,' he said stubbornly. 'The first one is that I love you. That I've loved you all these years. That I'll *never* stop loving you, Marne.'

A startled look flashed across her face. She put both hands up to cuddle his face, and looked straight into his dark eyes. 'I wish it could be true,' she said, sighing.

'It is,' he assured her. 'It is the absolute truth.' Two more tears appeared in her grey-green eyes, and slowly dribbled down her cheek. He stopped their flow with his finger. Her infinite strength broke down, her stiff backbone collapsed, and she fell across his shoulder, crying her heart out. For five minutes he let her cry, and when the tears were gone he climbed to his feet and pulled her up after him.

'It was a job that had to be done,' he told her. 'I haven't been off lawyering for the past four years. I took a job with the Federal Bureau of Investigation—the FBI. Are you listening?'

One of her slender hands came up around his neck and locked itself into the hair at the nape fo his neck. It was the best acknowledgment he could expect. The saliva began to run in his dry-as-dust mouth. He moved his head, and his lips gently touched hers. Just a touch, but it was not refused.

'This county,' he went on, 'has been one of the most crime-ridden counties in the nation. So the director set up a political sting operation. I was to come back and run for office, working my way into the Burroughs machine all the time. You've seen some of my men—accountants, lawyers, detectives. We've amassed enough evidence to break the machine completely. Yes, I know it all constitutes a sort of lie, but it was worthwhile, don't you think? Burroughs himself is in jail. About five of his cronies got away. One of my people made a slip—to Sylvia Burroughs—would you believe that? And she blew the works yesterday afternoon.'

'I'll believe anything,' Marne whispered.

'Then—you'll listen?'

'Is there more?'

'There's always more,' he told her. 'I love you, Marne. That's why I was eager to come. I wanted you to know— the fake marriage was no part of the Bureau's scheme. I set that up for myself. And as far as I'm concerned, love, it was no fake. Everything was legal, including the fact that the groom loves the bride.'

And the bride loves the groom, Marne thought. Always has, always will. One of her hands escaped the crush, and wandered to the collar of her dress, where the little blue sapphire sparkled in that light of the lamp beside her chair. There was so much left to be explained. She slumped, and he lowered her back into the chair.

'You treated me like some kid,' she accused.

'Then? Not now. I know better. We'll go on as partners.'

'Equal?'

'Well, I don't know about that,' he said, chuckling. 'There were times when I felt pretty well put down. Would you allow me to be equal?'

A tiny flash of a grin ran across her face, and was gone. 'No more dictatorship?'

'No more.'

'You were gone so often that I hardly ever saw you at night.'

'Yeah. Crazy,' he admitted. 'It was that crazy thing about amateur theatricals. We all thought that we were the coming things in theatre arts. It took us almost a year to find out that it wasn't true.'

'But—you could have told me. I could have come with you—'

'I didn't dare tell you. You would have laughed your head off.'

'Which just goes to show you didn't know me as well as you thought. I would have come. And I wouldn't dream of laughing.' A pregnant pause.

'Nothing else,' he asked.

'Babies,' she said. 'I wanted a baby, and you—'

'And I wouldn't allow it? Because I was too selfish, Marne. Because I wanted you all to myself. Because I was just beginning to find myself in the law business, and wasn't making a great deal of money. Because I thought—that we were both too young.'

'There's one more problem,' she said. She got up from the chair like an old woman, creaking in all her joints, waving aside his offer of help. 'No, I have to do this for myself.'

When she came back she was clutching the videotape that had haunted her for so many years. Clutching it so tightly that her fingers had turned white.

'Can I help?' he offered. She waved him off.

'Just sit there,' she said.

He took the rocking-chair. She marched over to the sofa, and the coffee-table next to it. All her VCR equipment was there. She turned it on, then inserted the tape.

'Watch,' she commanded. 'Just watch.'

The TV set warmed up just in time to catch the lead-in of the tape. For five torturous minutes the tape ran, showing shadow figures wrestling on a worn couch. Sex play, as explicit as one might ever see, ending just as he was stripping the formal gown from the girl. From Sylvia Burroughs. And the man was Rob Smith. She watched the screen in silence as the tape ran out, and then she turned to him.

'Well?'

'Not as well as you might think,' he said. But he was laughing as he said it. Not just smiles, but outright laughter.

'You think that's funny,' she snapped. 'I thought it was adultery.'

'You're not serious, Marne? I think it's funny as hell.'

'I didn't,' she mumbled. 'I thought it was as serious as hell when I got it. That's when I went down and filed for divorce.'

'You mean to tell me that we've been apart for four years because of this little piece of tape? My God, woman, you—'

'Yes, I did,' she said firmly. 'For this little piece of truth. I don't believe I've heard you deny it. It's true, isn't it? You and Sylvia Burroughs?'

'Oh, Marne!' he exclaimed as he pulled her into a hug. 'All those years over this? This is what set the fire?'

'This is it.' She turned her head to one side and rubbed it into his light sweater. He must not see me cry, she told herself. Must not!

'And if it hadn't been for this tape?'

'I would have struggled to put up with the rest of it. But this—no woman could put up with this.'

'If I could prove to you that it's not what you think?'

'Don't torture me, Rob,' she yelled at him, pounding against his chest with both little hands. 'If you could prove it wasn't true I'd...' And the tears doubled. He found a handkerchief and offered it. She accepted, stepping back from him, dabbing at her eyes.

If he could prove it not to be true? Marne grappled with her conscience. Of course, it *had* to be true. There it was in full colour, right in front of her eyes. But if it wasn't? How could she deny what she felt? If it was not true— 'I still love you, Rob. I won't live with you, but I still love you. If wishes could make it all go away, it would be gone. Someone sent that to me. Brought it, not mailed it. I found it in the morning when I opened the door to get the paper.'

'Marne, Marne.' He cherished her closely, lifting her a little off her feet so her head would lie on his shoulder. 'Marne, I can prove that this is just another lie. Will you grant me the time?'

'Yes. Lord, yes,' she muttered as he gently set her aside.

'I have to go over to my mother's house,' he said. 'I want you to wait right here. Watch the television. The polls have closed. They'll be reporting the counts pretty soon. With county-wide machine ballots, we ought to know the results very soon.'

'All right.' But instead of watching the television she watched him as he went back into his room, came out, made a bathroom stop, and went out of the front door.

Morgan came to join her. The old cat tried to jump from
the floor into her lap, but her time had gone for gymnastics.
She considered the situation, then walked around to the side
of her chair to where the sewing basket rested. Using the
basket as a mid-point, she jumped—and made the distance.

Marne's hand dropped on to the cat's head as she rubbed
back and forth. The cat hummed. Her stub of a tail wagged
portentously. 'I don't care *what* he brings back,' Marne
said. 'No matter what. I'm going to believe him. I'm going
to, even if it's the biggest lie in the world. That shows you
what a marshmallow *I* am.' Morgan offered a noisy agreement before settling her magnificent head and nudging for
more petting.

Marne reached up with her free hand and found her sapphire gift. 'Blue for fidelity,' she murmured. 'Lord help me
to believe!'

It was close to eleven o'clock before he came back. His
car roared up to the front of the house, and made a squeal-
ing stop. Marne held to her chair, flashing a look to the
ignored TV. And then broke out into a full smile.

'Well,' he said as he came in. 'That's a good sign.'

'What?'

'You're smiling.'

'With good reason,' she said quietly. 'What kept you?'

'I couldn't find it,' he said, shaking his head in disgust.
'My mother didn't appreciate it, so she put it away in the
attic along with the other junk she's been accumulating.'

He was carrying an old plastic bag. A fumbling moment
later he brought out—another videotape. 'Now it's your
turn to watch.'

Marne smiled at him. Of course, she was going to watch.
Even though she believed already whatever it was he
wanted to tell her. 'Is the moon actually green cheese?' she
asked.

'What?'

'The Moon. Cheese,' she repeated, smiling.

He paused and stared at her as if trying to read between the lines. And then, 'Yes, the moon is made out of green cheese. You believe that?'

'I believe that,' she admitted.

'Then wait till you see this,' he said, chuckling. He snapped the switch, and the tape began to roll, overriding the election TV programme. The title on the videotape was somewhat distorted. 'The Odeon Players,' it said, 'present *Murder in the Living-Room.*'

And for fifteen minutes Marne stared as an obviously amateur group of players stumbled through their lines and over the stage furniture, telling the story of a murder at Thacker Heights. Just when she was getting interested Rob stopped the tape.

'Now this,' he said, 'is the interesting part.' He set the tape in motion again. The scene shifted, through a squeaky door, into a living-room, and then, to her surprise, the identical scene rolled, the one she had kept to herself for all those years. It rolled to the point where her tape had ended, and then a few turns more. The loving couple separated, a door slammed, a gun fired off-stage, and Sylvia Burroughs fell dead on the floor.

'Well, that's enough,' Rob said as he shut down the VCR. 'I told you we have amateur dreams. We made three copies of this awful tape and mailed one of them to each of the three networks. I can't tell you the words they used when they mailed them all back. And then someone extracted this scene and sent it to you.'

'And someone did,' she said. 'And I believed it. Every lying inch of it. What a fool I was.'

He walked across the room and pulled her up out of her chair. 'No, not with all the other stuff that was going on,' he said. 'You had good reason. I was too full of ambition to look after you, and we were both too young to know better.'

'But now, Rob?'

'I want you back, to be my wife, to be my love. I can't say for sure that nothing like all that old stuff might never come up again. But I *do* say that if it does all you'll need to do is say the magic word to make it stop. If you'll have me.'

'Rumpelstiltskin,' she said.

'What?'

'Don't you remember? That's the magic word.'

She was up in his arms before she recognised what was going on. Into his arms, and out to her bedroom. Things were in good shape. She had taken some of the last twenty-four hours to strip and clean and re-shape. He lowered her to feet. She stood there smiling as he began to unbutton and unbuckle. She shivered as the last little wisp of silk fell to the floor.

'Cold?'

'Anticipation,' she stuttered.

'There's a cure for that,' he said.

'I was sure you would know of one.' Her fingers were busy as she told him. Cold, shaking fingers, struggling with strange buttons and curious zips, until they were both nude.

'Me Wolfman,' he said as he picked her up and threw her on the bed. The springs bounced her around for a moment, just long enough for him to join her. 'Me Wolfman,' he repeated.

'Let's have a little less talk and a little more action,' she commented primly. And he provided it.

Through the long night there were strange noises in the bedroom. Morgan came in twice to protest. At her age, the cat needed her sleep. All through the long night, and then silence.

He awoke with the sun in his eyes, and the thunder of the old grandfather clock sounding thirteen. Thirteen? The bed space next to him was empty. Twisted sheets, pummelled pillow, but empty. He rubbed his chin. A shave was in order. In fact, Marne probably needed medical treatment for wrestling with this gorilla. From out of the kitchen he heard voices. Female voices. Two.

He came up out of the bed like a soldier, ready to run or hide as might be. On the floor in one corner he found a pair of his trousers and a shirt, and one sock. The other was long gone. So he climbed into trousers and shirt and went stalking out into the kitchen, barefoot. The linoleum was colder than he had expected.

'G'mornin', Uncle Rob.' His niece Becky, dressed in neat, clean dungarees, a blouse, and sandals. Neatly dressed.

'Good morning, Becky.' He patted the top of her head and smiled at Marne, at the stove.

'Good morning, Marne.' She turned in his direction, a smile on her face and a lively twinkle in her eye—and a touch of white lotion rubbed liberally into her cheek.

'Combat pay,' she said. 'I demand combat pay. Eggs? Bacon?'

'What's that mean?' Becky interjected. 'Combat pay?'

'It's a game we were playing last night,' Marne said. 'A sort of Nintendo game for grown-ups. I was only teasing him.'

'I'll have eggs,' he said. 'Sunny side up. And toast. No bacon. I'm trying to cut down on my cholesterol count.'

'Great idea,' Marne said, chuckling. 'That means you have to cut out the eggs first. They're the worst things you could eat.'

'What does that mean?' Becky again.

'It means that your uncle is getting old,' Marne said solemnly. 'He has to watch his diet and all that sort of good stuff.' A pert appraisal, just for a moment, and then, 'You look tired, Rob. Didn't you get enough sleep?'

'No, I didn't,' he said sharply. 'And, after certain ears around here are removed, there'll be a reckoning.'

'What does *that* mean?' Becky asked.

'That doesn't mean a thing,' Marne returned. 'The poor old fellow is too weak to do almost anything, and he knows it. Here are your eggs, Rob. We'll use up the ones we have, and then get a substitute for them. I know that some organisation makes liquefied eggs without the yellow in them. That's the part that has the cholesterol.'

'I wish it could be quieter around here,' Rob said with his best dignity showing. 'It's—nine o'clock, and I'd like to hear the news. Which reminds me. How come that grandfather clock strikes thirteen?'

'It always does,' Becky volunteered. 'Been doing it for years.'

'Here's a local news station,' Marne said, and flipped the switch on the radio. The announcer was in full flight. 'And despite the fact that the Burroughs ticket was shot down in flames, the neophyte candidate, FBI Agent Rob Smith, won the nomination on the Democratic Party ticket. Since there were no Republican candidates who might run against him in the November elections, it would appear, barring a miracle, that Mr Smith is the new county sheriff.'

'Oh, my God,' Rob said as he burned his mouth trying to drink his coffee too fast.

'That does make a problem, doesn't it?' Marne said in her sweetest voice. 'What do we do? Move to Washington, or run in the finals?'

'I haven't any idea what the Bureau will say,' Rob said. 'I was told to *enter* the primaries, not *win* them.'

'You can't go to Washington to live,' Becky said. 'Or if you do you'll have to leave Marne here. I need her worser than you do.'

'Worser?'

'It's a holiday. Worser is a perfectly good word for holidays!'

'Please, Becky, your uncle is having a stroke.'

'I guess I'd better call Washington,' Rob said.

'How about Sylvia?' Marne said, interrupting his chain of thought.

'Sylvia? What about Sylvia.'

'You said she got away.'

'She did. Went sailing off into the sunset, via TWA airlines. And cleaned out her dad's cash box. Which is why we were able to catch him on the fly!'

'That's terrible,' Marne said. 'She was the guilty one. I wanted very much for you to catch her and send her off to gaol for fifty years.'

'What, for stuffing ballot boxes?'

'Well, no. She's the one who sent me that—tape. For which she deserves fifty years in jail. Or worse.'

'Or worser,' he asked.

'Or worser. Look, Becky, you've had your breakfast, and there are some things your uncle and I have to settle. Why don't you scoot home? They'll excuse you for skipping one day of school, but no more. Off you go.'

The little girl gave them a solemn look, and then grinned. 'I know what you're up to,' she giggled. 'You want to decide which one of you will be sheriff!'

'And isn't that a fine idea?' Rob said as he walked to the door with his arm around Marne. They watched the little girl skip up the hill, and out of sight.

'And now,' Marne said firmly, 'we have to talk about cabbages and kings and sheriffs, and things like that—in the bedroom.'

'Oh, please,' Rob begged, 'not that.' With which he swept her up in his arms and carried her right to where she wanted to go.

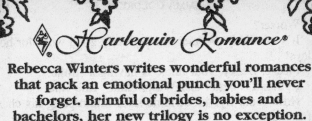

Harlequin Romance®

Rebecca Winters writes wonderful romances
that pack an emotional punch you'll never
forget. Brimful of brides, babies and
bachelors, her new trilogy is no exception.

Meet Annabelle, Gerard and Diana. Annabelle and
Gerard are private investigators, Diana, their
hardworking assistant. Each of them is about to face a
rather different assignment—falling in love!

LOVE
undercover

Their mission was marriage!

Books in this series are:

March 1999 #3545
UNDERCOVER FIANCÉE

April 1999 #3549
UNDERCOVER BACHELOR

MAY 1999 #3553
UNDERCOVER BABY

Available wherever Harlequin books are sold.

HARLEQUIN®
Makes any time special ™

Look us up on-line at: http://www.romance.net

HRLU

If you enjoyed what you just read,
then we've got an offer you can't resist!

Take 2 bestselling love stories FREE!

Plus get a FREE surprise gift!

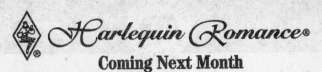

Coming Next Month

#3555 THE BOSS AND THE PLAIN JAYNE BRIDE
Heather MacAllister
Jayne Nelson feels her life lacks pizzazz. She's just spent her twenty-eighth birthday working overtime for her accounting firm. Then Garrett Charles walks into her life. Talk about pizzazz! Though Jayne realizes he's out of her league, that doesn't stop her daydreams becoming X-rated! But Jayne wants more than dreams...

#3556 TO CLAIM A WIFE Susan Fox
Caitlin Bodine is the black sheep of her family—and Reno Duvall certainly blames her for his brother's death. For five years, he's cut her out of his life. Now he's forced to share his ranch with this beautiful, heartless woman. He doesn't like it one bit, and neither does Caitlin. Only, living together, they discover how they've misjudged each other. Reno wasn't looking for a wife, but he becomes determined to claim Caitlin for his own...

Rebel Brides: *Two rebellious cousins—and the men who tame them!*

Meet Caitlin and Maddie: two beautiful, spirited cousins seeking to overcome family secrets and betrayal. As they come to terms with past tragedy, their proud, rebellious hearts are tamed by two powerful ranchers who won't take no for an answer!

Look out in July for To Tame a Bride.

#3557 THE PARENT TRAP Ruth Jean Dale
Matt Reynolds finds Laura Gilliam infuriating—and the feeling is more than mutual. Unfortunately, their kids have decided that they'd make a perfect match! But though Matt realizes that his little girl needs a mother and Laura that her little boy needs a dad, they're determined not to fall into the parent trap! But is it too late?

#3558 FALLING FOR JACK Trisha David
Jack Morgan has been left to bring up his small daughter Maddy single-handedly. It wasn't easy. Then Bryony Lester fell into their lives. Maddy warmed to her instantly—how could Jack resist a woman who could make Maddy smile?

Daddy Boom: *Who says babies and bachelors don't mix?*